p.s. A Edizione

per sempre Anita edizione
Via delle Scienze, 17 Ferrara 44100

ALSO BY SANDRO DARIOSTO

THE LAST GOOD RUN

BURTON THE RED
An omnibus edition

BURTON WITH THE THOUSAND

IN THE NORTH

BEYOND ASPROMONTE

and forthcoming from *per sempre Anita Edizione*

THE WISDOM RUN

HANDS OF THE BIRD

HANDS OF THE BIRD

& Other Stories

Sandro Dariosto

per sempre Anita Edizione
Ferrara Seattle
2016

Selected stories in this volume previously appeared first in slightly
different form in HARPER'S FERRY REVIEW and THE SEATTLE
REVIEW.

This is a work of fiction. Names, characters, places, and incidents
are either the work of
the author's imagination or are used fictitiously.

Library of Congress Control Number: 2016949818
per sempre Anita Edizione, Redmond, WA

Printed in the United States of America

per sempre Anita Edizione
via delle Scienze 17 Ferrara

10 9 8 7 6 5 4 3 2 1

For the Sweetness of the Honeybee

Contents

Hands of the Bird
& Other Stories

Death and the Freedman

. . . it's simpler, in fact, not to want to be free . . .
James Baldwin
Nobody Knows My Name

The rain began to fall steadily when the train whistle blew, as if there was a connection between the two. Robert grabbed a cold iron handle on the boxcar and, throwing his foot up onto a bracing, pulled himself into the dark car. He closed and bolted the door behind him to keep the damp air out, and he heard the whistle of the Texas Rover blow again in short bursts. With the door closed, the freight car was already into the night.

He sat back on the one hard bench and rested his head against the wall. Closing his eyes and folding his arms over his chest, the heat in his body surged back against the chill air, and he listened to the rain drumming gently on the car. It would be a good night for sleeping, he thought. Against the back of his head he felt the rumble of the train starting to move; it shook his whole skull and loosened his jaw until his mouth fell open. Then he let out a slow, comfortable yawn.

They called the engine the Texas Rover, and it was taking him deep into Texas in the late winter of 1915, to a piece of land he had bought all his own. With his eyes closed he could see the Rover spit black coal smoke and hiss white steam and turn her seven wheels on each side. She was pulling him, hauling Robert Mahon to his freedom. And marked out in fancy letters on the side of every car shone the A. T. & S. F. The Atchison, Topeka, and Santa Fe.

The whistle blew again, a long burst, but distant now through the walls and the rumble of the rolling train.

"Yesss-sir," a voice hummed out deep and low, "I do loves the sound of a train whistle."

The freighter began to rock just then. Robert opened his eyes and saw nothing but the dark. Slowly the rain's drumming faded away, obliterated by the pounding of the freight car on the track.

"Evening, sir," the voice said. Then there was a long uneasy silence. Cars rattled noisily over a break in the rails, and the whistle blew again. "Trains make a nice wail, don't you think? Sir?" the voice said.

But Robert didn't answer. Gradually he made out an old, gray haired, black man sitting amongst the baggage and freight at the other end of the car. His head was bent low, and Robert sensed the man was being cautious around a stranger.

Suddenly a baritone chuckle echoed around the boxcar like something whispered in a well. "Am I so black you can't see me in the dark? Sir?" the old man said.

"No. No, I can see you fine. You just surprised me. I was the only one in here when we stopped."

The old man's chuckle rolled out into a laugh then. He wore a tattered wool coat that hung to his waist, and he held his head bent down just inches above his knees. Robert kept waiting for him to sit up straight; the position he sat in looked damned painful.

The old man shook his head while he laughed and the laughter seemed to relax him some. He seemed to have the measure of Robert Mahon, and he loosened up a little then. "I bet you never seen a niggruh before, have you?" he said.

Robert was going to deny it, but when he looked that old man in the eye he had to admit it. "You know," he confessed. "When you get right down to it, I guess I haven't."

The black man grinned broadly. "I know I's not the best example of my people, but I'm Isaac Waters, sir." Robert noticed the old man's pants were gray and cotton, and splitting below one knee, and they were clearly too big for him.

"Robert Mahon," he nodded his head and shifted forward on the hard board seat.

"Glad to meet you, Mister Mahon. I thought this old gentleman might have to ride alone tonight." His head bounced a touch as he talked. "You know," he said, "freight cars on rainy nights can get some loneliness in them, Mister Mahon."

Isaac Waters had one foot in a crusted black shoe propped up on a canvas traveling bag, and he was leaning forward with his head and shoulders bent down near his knee. He looked like he was trying to tie his shoe, but he just leaned that way and had to twist his head back to look across the car at Robert. He sat on a flat tin trunk and his other leg disappeared down into the sacks and crates and carpetbags around him. The gray hair on top of his head was a soft, clear spot fading away into the black of his face, and of the railcar's inside.

"Where you headed?" Robert asked, thinking of the next two days on this train, sitting in this freighter, and even as odd as this old colored fellow was, liking the idea of a little company and conversation along the way.

The gray spot of his head turned up and the old man, smiling from between his shoulders, said, "I don' know for sure. Kansas City, maybe." His head lowered a touch. "I's raised in Kansas City, I was. Though I don't suppose anybody will remember. If anybody's even there. But I like Kansas City," he said. "Almost like home to me," he said.

Robert Mahon had never in his life gone anywhere without knowing almost to the hour when he'd be back. That is, until he left this time for Texas. But this old colored man here wasn't even sure where he was going, much less when he'd get there, and Robert liked that. He liked knowing there was someone else wandering out here, someone else taking a chance on what was over the next hill.

So he asked, "Where'd you leave from?"

Isaac Waters snorted again. "I been in Chicago a long time. Long enough." He paused before he named the city and then said it quickly dropping the whole first syllable into a grunt. "Chucawgo," he said, and then he laughed. "You all wouldn't happen to have some hooch with you, would you, Mister Mahon?"

"Pardon?" Robert sat up straight. He felt the edge of the hard seat on his back.

"Would you have any liquor on you, Mister Mahon, sir?" The old man's voice was more careful this time.

"Oh. No. No, I never thought of it."

Isaac Waters laughed, and then he sounded more strange and colored to Robert with every word he spoke. He began to sound like the black-face comics that passed through Iowa when Robert was a boy. "Ol' Isaac, he don' mean to shif' on you so quicks there, suh. I's jus' one thirsty niggruh, dat's all, suh."

Then he reached down into a canvas sack between his legs and pulled out a flask. It was nearly full of something the color of wet clay. "Say, how bouts that. I guess I broughts a little of my own," he said, pulling out the cork and taking big gulp, swishing the liquor around in his mouth before he swallowed. After he had relished the taste, he asked, "Would you care for a little shot, sir?" The vaudeville accent was gone

"Sure," Robert Mahon said, feeling a strange camaraderie in the drink. He got up and walked across the car. As he came near, the old man twisted his head farther back on his shoulders and lifted a knee, so he could lean back and look up without changing the angle of his backbone. Robert took the bottle from his outstretched hand. "Thank you, Mister Waters," he said.

The old man glanced up at Robert's face when he heard that "mister." But he just grinned. "Isaac. Isaac's the name, sir," he said, as Robert took a long swig from the flask

That swallow of liquor rode down through Robert's chest and into his gullet like a spill of burning kerosene. He sucked in a deep breath like he was going under, and then Robert heard that baritone chuckle again, while he tried to get his wind back. "You like that?" Waters said, before Robert could speak.

"Shit, that stuff's dangerous," Robert muttered in one burst, once he could. "What is it?"

"That's good old, home brewed Negro whiskey, my friend," Waters laughed. "It makes the Scotch and the Irish call for help."

Isaac Waters stood up then.

"That's just a little of Pappy June's hooch, suh," he said. "Finest concoction on the whole of the South Side."

He stepped out from the baggage then, and Robert got his first good look at the whole length of this man. It was one sight Robert never would forget. Isaac Waters hobbled over to the boxcar door and opened it a crack. Even standing, his spine never straightened out completely. The foot that was hidden until then was really just a stump. A large boot, with the toe cut off and the hole left by it sewn shut, was strapped onto the end of Waters' leg. If there was a whole foot in that shoe, it was a twisted one.

But, despite the way he looked, the old man scrambled around with ease. He moved the way a caged animal does, stiff and disjointed, but apparently without pain. He leaned onto the side of the door and thrust his gut out as far as he could. It looked ridiculous, his bent shoulders traveling out farther than his crotch, but Isaac Waters made the move with practiced ease.

"I do hate to run this through me so fast. Lord only knows when Ike'll see another bottle of Pappy June's good stuff." Robert made a mental note not to use that side of the door, when he climbed into the car later. "I never could hold anything," the old man said. Isaac Waters chuckled and pulled himself in, closing the door of the car. Then he limped back to Robert and said, "Friends call me Ike." He stuck out his open hand.

Robert thought a moment before he took that hand, remembering where it had just been. But then they shook hands, and Robert smiled. "Glad to meet you," he said. "Ike."

"It's my pleasure, Mister Mahon, sir," Ike Waters said, and then the old black man added, cautiously, "Robert?"

Robert Mahon nodded his head. "Robert," he said. "Robert."

An hour or two passed by in a rush, filled with Ike Waters' tall tales from Chicago, and with the rattle of steel wheels on steel rails. But then there came a rare pause, and the old man fell silent.

"So where you headed?" Ike asked him, after a moment.

"Texas," Robert said. It was true, just saying the word out loud still thrilled him.

"Well," Waters said. "I lived some months in Texas once. Where in Texas you going?"

"The Valparaiso," Robert said. He sat back against a crate and settled into the shimmying of the boxcar through the seat of his pants, and talked about wheat and cattle and two hundred acres. "All I could manage in Iowa was to rent eighty, Ike," he said. "But I got two hundred acres of prime Valparaiso grassland that are all my own now. By God," he laughed and set his head back against a strut on the wall.

"Land's a nice thing to have, Robert," the old man said. He paused and thought about something for a moment. "It ain't everything though. No sir. I say it ain't everythin'."

There was flat silence then while Robert wondered what he meant by that. What could be wrong about owning your own land?

"I never heard of no Valparaiso. Where the hell is it?"

Robert drew a map on the floor with his fingernail, and that map looked about as much like a cow's udder as it looked like Texas. But it would do. With his thumb he rubbed around the spot in the southwest, and tapping the floor he called it the Valparaiso.

"Never heard of it," Ike said again. But the old man pointed, with a hand as dark as the floor, at the northern part of the state, near the panhandle.

"I spent most of one summer 'round there," Ike said. "'Yano Stackado' they called it. Mile after mile of the thickest grass 'n the rollingest hills, 'n the hottest damned Augusts.   Least ways that summer."

"What were you there for?"

"Farming," Ike said. "I was staying with my Aunt Eulah and my Cousin Boss. I was just a boy then, about ten or eleven.   Mama sent me down there from K. C.   Right after the War 'tween the States, you know?"

"Ike, that's fifty some years ago." Robert took another, closer look at him. Waters seemed old, but sort of ageless too. He didn't look like any man in his sixties. He was lean and hard, and agile for a crippled man.   Robert found himself wondering about the years of deprivation and fight that must have made this man of sixty look ten years younger than his age, made him look like he could limp and drink hooch and laugh about it all forever.   Or maybe it was easy times that made him so ageless.

"Boss moved out to Texas from Louisiana, right after the war ended. Just like you, he wanted to have himself a farm.   Just him and Aunt Eulah. At that time Mama was washing sheets, she was the laundry maid, for some white folk in Kansas City, for the Polks.   Mr. Polk, he owned a big chunk of some railroad, so he told Mama he'd send me down there to the country for the summer, and maybe longer. I guess Mama thought it would do me some good."   He was gazing down past his twisted shoe on the floor.   "Or maybe them folk just wanted me out of their hair. I don't know.

"But I rode on down there in an empty cattle car, Robert, and it wasn't half as nice as this here little side-door Pullman, no sir." The old man pointed his finger sprightly all around in the air. "There was holes in the roof of that car, 'n it rained harder than this all the way to Amarillo," he said. "I's supposed to be Boss's help for the harvest." Then Ike laughed, long and alone and dark as a tunnel. A different laugh than Robert Mahon had ever heard before. "The harvest," he said softly again.

That word, mixed with the sound of Ike's dark laughter, landed on Robert's ears uneasily. "Well, what was it like down there?" he said.

"You want to hear the whole thing? If not, I just say that harvest went to the crows, 'n let it rest."

"I've got lots of time," Robert said slowly, waving a hand at the freighter around him.

Ike Waters hesitated, ran his tongue across his lips. "It was a different time then," he said. "Things was looking up, they were, back then."

But he wouldn't tell all of his story that night. No matter what Robert said. He told part of it here and part of it there, part of it in Missouri and parts in Oklahoma, and some even in the dry Texas sun. Whenever the night turned darkest, when the rumble of the train seemed loud and ugly, Ike Waters would talk about Boss and Eulah. Slowly, with freight train time, the pieces of the story came together in Robert's mind. So in years to come when Robert Mahon remembered Ike Waters, it seemed to him this story was one piece of whole cloth, and not a quilt with ragged edges. He remembered Ike telling the story this way:

The old man scratched at the furrows in his forehead, using all the fingers of one hand. After he sat a long while in thought, he said, "When I came down there Boss had a nice, pretty little vegetable garden, 'n he had a big field of corn. That was his cash crop, he called it. He was going to sell it off in the fall and buy himself a good sow for the winter, be raising pigs come spring. And Boss had one other thing. He had the orneriest damned mule in the Union; some government slicker give it to him. Jezebel was its name," he chuckled, "sweet as could be till you wanted that mule to do something."

"Did this Cousin Boss run a farm?" Robert asked. "Back in Louisiana?"

There was a moment then when Robert wondered if Ike was going to answer him. "I guess you too young to remember, ain't you, Robert Mahon," Waters said eventually.

"Remember what?"

"Eulah was the cook. Cousin Boss, he was the head butler at some big house in Baton Rouge." The black man stopped there, with a sharp nod of his head as if to settle the point clearly in his own mind, then he said, "Boss 'n Eulah be slaves, Mister Mahon." He let the sound of that word settle in the dark of the rail car, and though there was no echo inside that empty space, for a while there seemed to be one.

"Boss knowed less than a pile of pigeon droppings about farming, and the only reason that garden was so nice was cause of Eulah. In

Louisiana, in them days, a cook knowed how to grow her own vegetables."

Robert tried to ignore that way Ike's voice rose as he spoke. But the black man spoke louder and quicker as he went further on into his memory. "But why did he go farming then?" Robert said.

Ike rubbed a finger across his nose roughly a couple times, and then he smiled. "Cause Andy Johnson give him forty acres and a mule, if he wanted it, Robert. And cause that felt a whole lot more like freedom than answering some white folks' door." He closed his eyes and laughed out loud, without much humor. "I knowed as much about farming as them two, and I never been outside of Kansas City back then."

Ike Waters took a pull on his flask of Pappy June and offered it to Robert. But Robert shook his head no. Ike took another, longer drink, and then muttered something Robert couldn't make out about slaves and masters, with a sneer on his face. They were the kind of words you didn't ask a man to repeat, Robert knew that from their tone. Ike seemed to forget he was talking to anyone in particular then.

"When I got down there to Texas, in the middle of July, things were sugar cane sweet, you know. First thing we done was drive Boss a new well. And that was all right, working together with our hands. Me 'n Boss. Him joking me all the time about whether my middle leg was like my crooked one or my straight one. Boss was a good man, he was. But then, one night, he was gone after supper for a long time, 'n Aunt Eulah started worrying. 'Now where is that man?' she kept saying. 'What's taking him so long?' I couldn't figure out why she was so keyed up. She started to waddle from one end of that shack they had to the other. But lucky for her, that wasn't too far. Cause Eulah be one big old woman. She was about the only thing out there that could rival the grass for being spread out.

"'Maybe he's out in the barn,' I said to her, cause I seen him going in there lots of nights. But she said she called him there just an hour before. 'Wouldn't hurt to go look 'n see, would it?' I said, not knowing what I was doing to that man. I just wanted to see what he be doing in there all the time, you know. By himself." Ike began to grin. His eyes squinted a little tighter and he looked away at the floor while he talked.

"It was after dark an hour or more so Eulah lit a candle stub 'n went out the door toward the barn. Of course, Boss's barn wasn't much. Just a ramshackle little hutch." Ike gently tucked the flask into the pocket of his coat, and patted the bottle once or twice affectionately, making sure it was snug and safe. "The onliest thing shakier than that barn was the fences Boss built. Old Boss he didn't take much to digging post holes. No sir." The old man's grin melted down into a frown then.

"What the hell I telling you this for anyway," he said bitterly.

"You don't have to tell me nothing," Robert said. "Nothing at all." But Ike Waters rested his forehead in his hands, and after a long silence, he went on.

"Even with this leg here I could move a lot quicker than old Eulah, so I got to the barn door a few steps ahead of her. When I opened that door, there was that high rolling Boss with his pants down to his knees, slouching bare assed across a bale. I stood there staring at him, trying to figure it out. It took him some time to get back from wherever his imagination was. When he turned and saw me, there was a look in his eyes I ain't seen in fifty years since." The old man shook his head. "Like shameful terror," he said, "poor old Boss."

"But Eulah, she shoved in front of me, 'n where Eulah shoved, Lord knows she went. 'Get back on up to the house, child,' she said to me. But what I seen got the better of any desire I had to obey that order. I kept trying to look around Aunt Eulah, but that's a whole lot easier to try than to do. Believe me. All I got to see after that was one big eyeful of Eulah's behind. I was twisting and squirming to get free, but she just held me tight behind her back." He laughed at the thought, and then he looked over at Robert Mahon.

Right then Robert didn't know what to think exactly, and he wasn't sure anymore that he wasn't being played for a fool. "What are you trying to tell me now?" he said, slowly, turning and cocking his head so he gazed down at Ike from an angle, as if his chin and his cheek could protect his eyes from some trick.

"There wasn't another black woman besides Eulah for at least three days ride on that mule, Mister Mahon," Ike said. He bellered out a laugh again, but this time it was impish and bright.

"I always figured Cousin Boss was only working with his hands in there. But I can not promise you, Robert Mahon, that some old bastard black calf ain't my first cousin," he said, leaning in toward Robert. "Once removed, of course." His big grin showed the gaps in his teeth.

"Aaah, hell with that shit. Who do you think you're playing with?" Robert said with a laugh. But Ike held out a gray palm, and whispered, "No, no, it's the God's truth, Mister Mahon. I swear. The God's own truth."

There was a distant rumble, like thunder miles away, then it rumbled closer to them, in a rhythm with the train. The two men listened, as the Texas Rover rolled over a section of bad track, until the rumble became a rattle under their feet. A red paisley bag fell to the floor with a thump.

"After that night, things were different down there, Robert. Boss only come up to the shack for breakfast and supper, 'n he started sleeping outside somewheres. Or maybe he was sleeping in the barn," Ike smiled at the thought. "Eulah would send me out to work with him everyday, but he never says nothing to me except 'Get over there 'n hoe that cornfield, nigger.' Believe you me. By the end of the week there wasn't a weed left on that whole farm. Things went on like that for some time, with the corn getting to be up over waist high, 'n with Cousin Boss stewing away by himself, day after day.

"A couple of weeks later, Boss decided we should plow up some of the prairie around his field. Breaking the sod for next year, he said. He got his little plowing rig all ready. 'N then he brought out Jezebel. That mule strutted right out of the barn pretty as a mule can, but once it got the harness on its back, and the plow behind it, the mule's true nature bean to show. That Jezebel would not move. She would not even budge.

"I was over in the garden, hoeing away contentedly, like a good boy, listening to Eulah humming and washing dishes in a tub. But I kept my eye on Boss 'n that mule. It was 'most funny for a time. Boss coaxed 'n he stroked 'n he patted that mule for almost half an hour, and Jezebel would not move. Then he tried to pull at her, and it would not move. Eventually he started yelling and shoving at it, 'n then he kicked it a few times. Once he kicked all the way up to Jezebel's ass. But the more he abused that mule, the more Jezebel decided not to budge. It was like every time he hit that creature, it growed roots.

"I guess Boss got pretty tired of that game 'fore long. He walked over 'n pulled a rail off the gate to his corn field. The whole fence line shook when he tugged that loose. He held that board up in front of Jezebel, 'n started brandishing it round. I guess one look at that would normally move a mule, but not Jezebel. That God damn beast stood and looked right back at him. With that dead look on her face. It's a good thing a mule can't smile, I tell you. Boss poked it a couple of times in the behind, but the only move Jezebel made was to kick the harness once or twice, letting Boss know he better stay clear if he wanted to keep his head.

"Right about then, I guess thirty some years of sorrows started pouring out of Boss. He swung back and struck that mule on the shoulders with the rail, 'n I thought he was done with it. Jezebel brayed out a coon dog shout. But then Boss went crazy, he started beating on that mule like it was made of solid rock. Like he thought he could bring water out of that stubborn as a stone mule. Jezebel bolted a couple of steps, but Boss just followed it right along, swinging that fence rail and beating that animal. I thought he was going to kill the poor thing."

"Christ Almighty," Robert said. Then he heard the old man clearing out his throat. "One time, Ike, I saw a man beat a dog, and the dog just crumpled up and took it. The poor thing didn't even run. It just gave up." The old black man spat what he got out of his throat onto the dirty floor. He set his bum foot out on a trunk in front of him, and he spoke looking at his flat, toeless shoe.

"Jezebel wasn't dumb enough for that, Mister Robert. No, sir. This mule bolted loose 'n headed straight for the cornfield. It leapt right over the gate where Boss had tore out his rail. Of course, that mule was still dragging a plow, and when that plow went on through, Boss's shaky fencing job come tumbling in like an old bundle of sticks. Jezebel set right in to tearing up the field then. Lord, what a mess that mule made," Ike stopped again, to shoot another wad of spit through his teeth at the floor. As he went on, his voice sank deeper and deeper into his baritone, and at times Robert had to listen close, and struggle to separate it from the low sounds of the train. "We had us a hell of a time trying to catch it. It was dreadful tough for a fat old woman 'n a gimpy legged kid to get hold of that mule. And Boss was no help, every time Jezebel looked at him, she'd wheel 'round 'n take out two more rows.

"It was Eulah finally got that mule stopped, but not until it was done with the field, 'n you can't tell me Jezebel didn't know what she was doing. There wasn't enough corn left in that field to throw my hoe at.

"I walked Jezebel back to the barn, making a wide swing clear of poor Boss. Nobody said nothing. Losing that crop that late in August was nothing nobody wanted to talk about. Boss just sat himself down in the new stubble over at the edge of his field. He sat there, 'n he didn't say a word to either of us for the rest of the morning. He just sat.

"'Leave him by hisself,' Eulah'd say. Over and over. 'Leave him alone now.' So I started picking up posts and the wire 'n putting that fence back together, though I don' know why. There wasn't nothing left worth fencing around. It was just something I could do,   'n Eulah went on inside. Boss just sat. He wasn't staring at nothing; he didn't even look worried. He looked like he just dumped a

load off his shoulders. If you'd a come walking along
'n seen him, you'd think he was just lazy, taking the
morning off.   In a couple hours, Eulah called out
that dinner was ready.   Boss got up, strolled over to
the barn. I watched for him till he come out with a
rope, 'n with Jezebel. Boss looked over at me 'n he
smiled, the first time he smiled at me since that
night in the barn. He say, 'Go on in 'n eat, Isaac. I
be there in a bit, son.'

   " 'Son.' That was exactly what he called me.
'Son.' Then he turn 'n walked out into the prairie
grass, with Jezebel trailing along behind."

   Ike Waters stood up then and stepped out of
the baggage around him. He put his hand on his
neck and rubbed at it, feeling for the pain. Then the
old man took another step forward, his bad foot
scuffed against the greasy floor, and he began to
limp toward the other end of the car.

   "While we was eating, Eulah talked about
some relative of ours, somebody I never heard of,
some cousin name of Oliver who be playing the
banjo and getting famous down in New Orleans.
She was doing her best not to mention Boss or the
field. But before long she got up 'n looked out the
door, and she say, 'I wish that man would come in
here 'n eat.' Then she saw he wasn't sitting in the
field anymore. She asked me where he was. I told
her about the rope 'n the mule. She just muttered
'Oh Lord' and asked which way they went. When I
pointed, she headed out that door faster than I seen
Eulah ever move. I tore off a chunk of the bread on
the table 'n watched her running from the doorway.

I just stood there and watched, thinking it was pretty funny, and wondering when I'd get back home to Kansas City, what with the corn crop ruined and everything. I was just a kid, Robert. What could I know?"

Robert leaned back against a tin-sided trunk, and he ran his thumbnail along the dirty grain of the floor. He glanced up now and then to watch the old man limping away from him, and he smelled the damp of the rain in the air. The night was turning bitter, right in front of his eyes.

"Old Eulah ran 'n ran till she disappeared behind a hill. I thought about leaving her alone with her child. But I was wondering too much about what he was doing with that mule. So I started running for that rise, too, chewing on my bread all the way. When I got to the top of that hill, I's surprised to find a tree. The only tree in Texas, I think. Down in the hollow behind that rise, where the rain waters would settle when it fell, there was an old white oak, not very tall but spread out wide as Eulah's bottom. Nearly."

Ike chuckled a touch, then he hobbled over to the hardboard bench nailed to one wall of the boxcar. It was the "immigrant seat." He sank down onto it like the old man he was, sucked in a long breath, and then told the rest of his story to the floor in front of him.

"Eulah was almost down to that tree. I could hear her panting. 'No, Lord, no,' she was saying over and over again. Jezebel stood down there, calm as a witness at somebody else's wedding, 'n when I looked closer, into the leaves of that oak tree, the bread dropped out of my hand and I started running down that hill as fast as this damned leg would let me.   See, Cousin Boss's feet were dangling down below the lowest branches of that tree.

"I ran down to that oak and looked up. Boss was hanging with the rope around his neck, his mouth 'n his eye were open, 'n his lips were turning blue. And his hands. Lord, I never will forget his hands. They were turned, palms out, with the fingers just a little curled.   It was like they were asking for something. Something none of us had.

"Eulah was climbing up the tree, 'n she was up high enough so about all I could see was up her dress. She was breathing so hard I thought she was going to die too.   She climbed up to where she could reach that man, and then up to the branch above the one he was hanging from. She jumped down onto that limb, 'n damn if it didn't bust.   Not all the way.   She had to kick it twice more, with poor Boss bouncing every time.   But she broke that branch clean off.   And it was oak, too.

"Boss fell out of that tree, bounced once on is back off one of the low branches.   I stretched him out on the ground, pulled the rope off his neck, 'n a big sigh went out of him that almost scared the crap out of me.   I felt heavy, like I was going to dirty myself.   By that time, Eulah was there hugging him 'n pounding on his chest, screaming, 'Lord, no' and starting to weep. Then, I'll be cursed if he didn't, all of a sudden, blink his eyes.   There was still some kind of fog behind them, 'n his lips was blue as half way down in hell, but he started breathing. He never said nothing, 'n he never moved his head. For about five minutes or so he moved his lips 'n eyes like a was trying to say something, but I don' think he was. He just looked like he was there, but he wasn't with us. In the end he stopped moving, 'n he was dead for sure underneath that tree, in the shade of that oak.

"Eulah 'n me buried him right there where he landed under that tree." Ike shook his head back and forth, in slow, empty rhythm with the train, but he never paused. "I carved his name deep as I could into the trunk of that tree. 'Benjamin Ossie Maltbia. 1832 to 1867 - One Tough Wasted Life. Amen.' That's what it said. It took me two whole days and a pair of blisters I can still find the scars from, but I carved that into that living tree. I stayed with Aunt Eulah then for a month or so, till the garden was all in 'n stored up. I tried to talk her into coming back to Kansas City with me. Mama wrote her a letter about it, one I had to read to her cause she never learned. But she wouldn't come. It wasn't till about a year later she finally gave in; she found out she couldn't live out there alone. That be no place for a lone woman."

Ike stood up and walked over to the door. "I think I better relieve myself again 'fore we get into town," he said. "I got the weakest bum of a bladder, one of these days I's gone drown myself from the inside. I swear."

He laughed, but while he stood at the door, he said, "Eulah used to go back there every year or so, on one of Mr. Polk's trains, just to visit that place. Part of some cattle ranch now, I think. There's probably bullshit all over the grave. I never been back there, though. I ain't been to Texas since." He lumbered back to sit beside Robert in the baggage, and the Texas Rover blew two more long bursts in the night.

Robert couldn't look at the old man for a while. The two of them sat in awkward silence. Robert's mind wandered outside, where the rain was pouring down on the parched ground; the water was taking out the winter freeze, and that gave him a warm feeling in the cool night.

"Ike," he said. "Jesus, Ike, don't take me wrong now. But I don't understand. Why did he do it, Ike?" Robert paused before he said, "It seems like a damn stupid thing to do, you know?"

"The branches of that tree were down low to the ground. Anytime, while he was hanging there, Robert, anytime at all that man could've put a foot out on one of those limbs 'n saved himself. Anytime," Ike Waters drew in a long slow breath. "Nobody ever knows why a man does that. He just up 'n do himself in one day. Then the rest of us, the ones left behind, we make up the reasons. And them reasons are just for us, Robert, because we don't know why. And that does scare us some. Because, you know, we don't know nothing."

Outside in the sleet, the train whistle let loose, and the Texas Rover began to slow down.

Ike Waters shook his head slowly back and forth. "You know, Robert, Eulah told me once that

Boss was the best 'n fittest butler in all of Baton Rouge. He could have made a good living, married up 'n raised children of his own, if he'd a just stayed in Louisiana."

Robert looked up from the floor at the bent old man and said, "What do you mean?"

"What I mean, Mister Mahon, is it be hard as dying for a man to say he make a better slave than a free man. That's a hard thing to say. There isn't nobody should have to say that to himself. But that was what Boss was doing. He was sitting in his field stewing on that, Robert. 'N he still be sitting 'n stewing on it somewheres."

Ike Waters sat, with his twisted back and his club foot, and he listened to the beat of the hard rain, returning through the murmur of the Texas Rover slowing down. "I wish to deepest hell I never saw Boss in the barn that night," Ike Waters said. Then he reached into his pocket, pulled out a match, and lit it with his thumbnail, holding it out before him in the dark car. In the match light he laughed, while it burned low and close to his fingers. When the yellow flame reached his thumb, it went out.

Hands of the Bird

It's much easier to talk about where you've come from than to say where you are going next.
Evan Parker, on
playing solo saxophone

One

I'm playing the streets again. I wail away on my tenor now in front of the Coliseum when the 'Sonics are in town. You can hear me outside the Kingdome on the yellow brick road when the Mariners play. I stay out of the rain in the winters here by playing under the awning at the Arena. Those are hockey nights, with good, rowdy crowds. Hockey fans toss bills in my case, you know, not just coins, man. My theory is hockey fans understand what it is to work in the rain, so they sympathize and they're generous, you know? But maybe they're just drunker.

I know what "street musician" means, too. It means you play next to the blind accordion guys and the tuba players doing Wagner charges and all those lame guitarists with some sad, old story to tell. But the people like tenor saxophones, you know, so I do all right. I make a pretty good living. And besides, baby, I get to play.

I've been thinking lately about making some changes, though.

There was a time once when I had my chances, man. Don't get me wrong. I lived with the world's most beautiful woman, and I played for people who listen, and know what they're listening to, you know. I was up there once, man. I was making music for the real bucks. I had my shot, but I guess I let it slip away, in the end. Maybe I let it go because it wasn't really mine.

You see, it all belonged to Bird, you know, or to Lucky anyway. It wasn't really mine.

You're probably not going to understand this and you'll probably think I'm nuts. But then you don't know what it is to be in the music. You don't know what it's like to be blowing there and suddenly you leave the changes and you're just out somewhere on a line that's coming through the horn, baby, coming through you, a pure line that's not yours, man, it belongs to the music, you know. It is what it is.

You wouldn't know about that. So how can I expect you to understand? How can you know what I lost out there?

Lucky walked up behind me and listened to me running the changes one night about a year ago. It was a shitty night. I mean, I was sounding pretty good. But some shortstop spiked the catcher and then all the players charged the field. There was big fight. When they broke it up, the Mariners lost the game anyway. So nobody was in the mood to pay the tenor man, you know, when they trudged out of the big dome. I was playing good, deep down blues, too. But it didn't matter. My case just rattled with a lot of dimes and the only bills inside it were the ones I put in there for seed. On top of everything else, it was starting to drizzle a slow Seattle rain.

And you know what? It was the end of that catcher's career, man. He ruined his knees, or something. And I can understand about that, babe. Believe me, I can understand about that.

But then Lucky walked up through the crowd that very same night. I noticed him right away, because he had a sort of 3/4 swing in his step. I knew he was a musician, man, by the way he walked. He was a tall, wiry black cat, over six feet. His face was sunken, like a black and gray skull. Except he had this little Clark Gable mustache, just a gray pencil line on his lip. He was wearing a neat, black suit with charcoal pin stripes that matched his mustache. I don't think, now, he was coming from that game. I think he was looking for a player, you know, to take over his burden. To lift it off him, man.

So he hung back behind me for a time, and listened, while I played hard and low down for that surly crowd who could have cared less. I played better than usual, too, because he was listening. But I didn't play anywhere close to where I soon could. Nowhere close, Jack. Nowhere.

His eyes narrowed as he heard me, and once he nodded. So I threw in a quote from "Pop Goes the Weasel" like Sonny Rollins, and he grinned. He got it.

When I stopped finally, he shook his head and said his name. "Lucky," he said. It might have been a jealous comment on my playing, but the way he said it I knew it was his name.

"You play?" I said. The people walked by, and they started to notice us. Like they hadn't when I was playing for them.

"Once," he said, his head bouncing in that 3/4. "I used to. I played alto, though, kid. No tenor for me."

"I thought you were a player, from the way you listened."

He smiled at something in his memory. "What's your name, kid?"

"Benny," I said. "Benny Crisp."

Then he looked directly in my eyes and said, "Come with me, Benny. I got something for you, Little Mister B. C."

Then he turned and started to stroll back down the yellow brick road, toward the stadium. I glanced around at the sour crowd spreading out into the parking lot and the streets, and I looked at the spare change in the case and felt the drizzle misting on my horn, and I thought to myself, 'Tomorrow is another day, right?'

Little did I know, back then.

So I slipped the neck off and slapped the horn in my case, and ran after Lucky with the case in one hand tinkling full of nickels and dimes, and with my mouthpiece in the other. He never looked back at me, and never said a word to me. He just bounded along in that gentle 3/4 of his, and I followed him.

The rain drizzled down a little harder and the crowd began to scurry in the wet. Still they seemed to part around Lucky. The sky was damp and gray when he led me down an alley toward some warehouses closer to the waterfront.

I was wiping the drizzle off my face when he stopped, suddenly. Lucky glanced both ways and then disappeared through an open door. I stepped inside this old brick building after him, and followed him into the dark. Or I followed the sound of his steps anyway.

"This way, Little B.C." he said. "I got something for you, boy." His voice came at me out of the darkness.

I wondered for a moment whether I was about to get jumped. A horn is worth some fast money, you know. You can hock it quicker than a watch, don't I know that now. But he just led me up a stairway into a loft, and then down a narrow walkway, where railings were all that hung between me and a long plunge down into the black warehouse full of crates and bins below us.

He opened what looked like an office door, and I heard some rats or something scuttle away. The vermin was clearing out, you know. Making room for us. I stepped inside his room, or his office, or whatever it was, and Lucky shut the door behind me.

"Long time ago, Benny, in a different place than this, there was a big time saint. You know what a saint is, son?"

"Yeah," I said. Everybody knows what a saint is, I thought. "They're the cats with them round golden hats on in all the old pictures," I said and laughed. He switched the light on then, and I saw sitting in the corner.   Not in a case or nothing. Just sitting there. It made me shut my mouth, man.

"A saint, Benny, is a guy who's got it, you know. He's got the gift, son, he's got that flame." Lucky snapped his fingers once then.   It sounded loud in the empty room. "He's a cat who can do without even thinking about it what the rest of us can only dream about trying. What you and I only wish about doing, he does it with out a thought, son." He stopped a minute and then laughed once, a little. "Dream about it, Benny." Then he laughed hard. "Dream," he said.

A bare yellow bulb hanging from a wire lit the room. There wasn't much else in that place, nothing but rat dust and cobwebs.   And the saxophone, sitting silent in the corner.

"A saint, Benny, has got the breath of life in his touch.   Listen close now, Little B. C. Listen to me. He's got it in his very fingertips, my man.   And people want it.   They know it, Benny, when they hear him breathe, they know he's got the gift. Hell, they'll fight amongst themselves over it.   Just to get close to it, just to be warmed by it. And if he lets them, they'll tear him to pieces for it. That's what can happen to a saint, Benny, if he lets them get too close."

Then Lucky stopped and held one of his palms up in the dusty air. "San Juan de la Cruz," he breathed out the name into the bare yellow light.

His teeth shone in his dark face. The Spanish words sounded funny and foreign coming from his lips.

But to hell with this weird old cat, I told myself, because I was looking at that horn, man. I knew it from across the room, baby, that was an old, brown, tarnished Selmer, man. A Mark VI in the lacquer, babe. In the original. It was the real thing. What it is, my friend. Sitting there loose and alone. I knew then why I'd been following this old fruitcake in pin stripes around in the dark. It was a horn, baby. A horn. A real horn.

"This was the cat's name, Little B.C.," Lucky lowered his head. " A long time ago, in a different place, Benny, when he died, they fought over him. San Juan de la Cruz, my man. He died in this one little burg they called Ubeda, but people wanted to bury him in another city. A place called Segovia, man. So they hauled his dead body across the country, with a horse and wagon, Benny. And little old Ubeda the burg, they weren't too happy about that, son. Not at all. The way they saw it, they were getting suckered. So, you know what they did? Little B.C.?"

I didn't answer him. I was barely listening to Loony Old Lucky. I was just eyeing that beautiful horn in the corner. I wanted to play it, you know. I would do anything he wanted, short of some kind of kinky shit, just to play that Mark VI. Even if it was an alto.

So I said, "What did they do, Lucky?" And I took a couple of steps across the room toward that sweet, old sax.

Lucky put a hand on my shoulder to stop me. "All along the road, Benny, every place they stopped with the body, the people wanted a piece of the Saint, kid.   San Juan de la Cruz. They wanted a relic, Benny, a piece of the poor dead Saint for themselves.   A scrap of cloth.   A lock of hair," Lucky laughed low down and paused. He touched my hair and I thought, 'Oh no, here it comes.'   But then he just pinched my ear lobe.   "An ear, Benny, or a toe.   Maybe a whole damn arm, son, or the old Saint's leg.   Everywhere they stopped, every little village and town, they took piece of him."

I twisted my shoulder loose and eased a few more steps toward the corner.   That Mark VI was like a magnet or something, man.   It was just there. I wanted to hold it, cradle it, blow it.   No, I got to be straight with you, man.   If I don't tell you the truth now, you won't believe me later. I wanted it. I wanted that horn. I wanted to possess it.

I set my sax case on the floor, and laid the Otto Link mouthpiece that was still in my other hand down on top of it.

"Segovia got his body, Benny. What was left of it, anyway. Madrid took an arm and little Ubeda got a whole damn leg.   Every little church and parish on the way there took a finger at least, Benny. They tore him apart, man. They ripped him up into little, bitty pieces."

"Where'd you get this horn, Lucky?" I said.   I walked all the way over to the corner and bent down to reach for the alto. "This is some nice old Selmer, my friend."

I'm going to be honest with you here. It was running through my mind just then how I could steal that Mark VI. Here I walked into this room, worried about losing my axe, and wound up planning how to jump an old man for his. The whole deal is pretty funny, considering where I am now. But this is what being in the music can do to you, man. It gets to be everything, you know. And sometimes you lose your mind over it. Not just your cool.

And if you let it, you can lose your life.

Just as I was about to touch that old, tarnished sax, Lucky said, "Benny?" It stopped me. I stood back up, and thought a little more clearly. He did say he had something for me. Maybe I wouldn't have to steal this beautiful horn in the corner.

"You said you got something for me, Lucky?" I looked over at his scrawny shape. He almost seemed to be fading away inside that pin-striped suit.

"Benny," he said to me, "do you know where Charlie Parker was when he died?"

His head tilted down a little and he gazed at me from beneath a knotted up brow.

"New York," I said. "Right?" I nodded at him and then bent back down and picked up that old alto horn.

"1955," Lucky said. "He was watching TV and his heart broke, son."

"Right. Something like that," I said. I was proud that I'd answered his little quiz. Maybe if I passed, it would earn me my little dream here. That's what I thought.

The Selmer was heavy. Now believe me, I'm used to standing around outside ballparks holding up a tenor sax, so I've hefted some weight. But this horn surprised me, man. It was weightier than just the metal, you know. That old horn was carrying some other shit, man. Something else was resting on it. Not just the lacquer.

"You know where they buried Charlie Parker, Little B.C.?" Lucky's head sunk even lower into his shoulders. "Do you know where Bird's grave is, son?"

The Selmer was all complete, right down to an old ivory mouthpiece and a reed. I loosened the ligature and slipped the old reed out, and it was some old piece of cane, man. That reed was as gray as the rats that lived with it, you know? Maybe even grayer.

"No, Lucky," I said. "Where is his grave? I don't know." I mumbled then, because I'd stuck that old reed in mouth and I was sucking on it. This is what that madness called the Music will do to you, Jack. It'll have you willingly sucking on old rat shit, hoping to soften it up. I'm telling you straight, my friends. You'll do it happily. You'll die to do it.

"He's buried in Kansas City, Little B.C.," Lucky said, and his head bounced now like I should have gotten the point. But I didn't.

Because I was setting that reed by then. I was eyeballing it under the bare bulb to be sure it sat nice and even next to the yellowing mouthpiece.

"So what you got for me, Lucky?" I said.

"Maybe you don't want it," he said.

I lifted the horn and ran my fingers up and down the keys, feeling the action. It was nice, man, like butter in the Alabama summer. Gently melting. If it blew half as good as it moved, this was going to be some kind of wonder horn.

"All the way from New York to K.C., Benny, they hauled him on the train," Lucky said.

I set my teeth on the mouthpiece and swallowed in a big breath. Then I blew. That old dead reed was still a little dry, but even so, this horn was sweet. It had a fat dark tone like a big oboe, but with the soft feel of a human voice at the edges. I blew just one long, low note for a while, and felt around with my embouchure for the ways that tone could change. It was tight and small, but a little shift of the lip and it would cry, or maybe growl. That was when I started to run the scales on it, to see where it could go and what it could do. It was solid, man, the same flex in the tone from the high F sharp all the way down to the low B flat. Without a squeak or a leak. It was fine, fine, so fine. A horn, baby. A real horn. A Sax-o-Phone. Call home on it.

So I started to play, and since we were talking about Charlie Parker, I slipped into a smooth and easy "Yardbird Suite." Lucky didn't smile or nod his head, but I was playing pretty good. Not bad for me. You know?

But like I say, it was nothing close to what I'd be playing in a week.

While I rode the changes through that tune, swinging it with a few yowls and field hollers, trilling a couple times on B flat and then slipping it into a blue growl, Lucky began to recite a list of names. He landed every name just a little ahead of my beat, and his little recitation began to drive my playing on. That list of names was making me swing. And what list it was, my friends. What names they were.

I swung along, keeping up as he dropped each name like a little bombshell on the tom-tom. "Stitt," he said. Then, "Art Pepper, Sonny Criss. "

It was hard to keep up though, as he went, because that horn seemed to grow heavier and heavier on me. It was taking all of my grit just to keep up with his beat. "Hank the Workout Man Mobley," he howled. I leaned back and held the horn up high, trying to staunch up my strength to keep on. "Long Tall Dexter too," he said.

But I found out I couldn't hold the horn up that way, not for long. So I let myself slip back down into a cool cat stoop. "And 'Trane had it too, Benny," Lucky said. Then he said, "Dolphy," in a beat or two, shaking his head back and forth, driving the swing a little quicker. I set the bottom of the alto on my thigh and tried to support it there, while I played along. But Lucky just swung on harder.

"Sonny the giant, the Old Newk," he shouted out. Then after a long pause, he whispered, "And Ornette too, Benny, Mr. Ornette too."

By that time I was bent way over low to the ground, holding that little horn just inches from the dirty boards I stood on, trying to keep it from falling to the floor. I had lots of wind, and the Mark VI played like a dream, but I just couldn't hold that sax up. Some kind of gravity was pulling that saxophone down out of my hands, out of my grip, back down to the floor.

"Let it go, Benny," Lucky said, shaking his head at me. "Don't be an idiot, Little B.C."

But I didn't really have a choice. That loaded alto was pulling me down onto my knees. It would drag me down and wrestle me flat onto the floor, I knew it would. So I stopped. I had to stop. I unhooked it from my strap and the horn fell sideways with a clatter on the boards in the dust.

"That's one hell of a sax," I mumbled. I looked up from my knees and saw old Lucky still shaking his head at me.

"Shit," he said.

But I still wanted that horn like I wanted a heartbeat Some foolishness never dies, man, like music foolishness. "Give it to me," I pleaded.

"Benny, Benny," Lucky gazed down at me like a scolding god, and ignored the little sax on the floor beside me. "Little B.C. Don't you know nothing, boy? You old enough to know, Little Benny, it ain't in the horn. By now you should know that, boy. The horn got nothing to do with it. It's in the soles of the feet, son, it's in the lungs and the heart, Benny, like some inherited disease. That's where it is, Benny. It's an infection. The horn be just the medicine that lets the infection breathe."

"Please," I said, but he shook his head no.

Lucky stooped down in front of me and easily picked up the old alto one handed, like it was some plastic toy. "Shit, Benny," he said.

"Give it to me," I said from my knees.

"Get up, boy," he said. He held the horn out in front of him, ready to play. But he didn't wear a strap, just held it there like it was some balloon and he wouldn't let it float away. "I got something real to give him, and Little Benny just wants this old saxophone." He spat those last three words out. I felt them like a hateful rain. "Get up," he said, almost yelling at me.

I stood, but my knees were weak now. That saxophone had drained something out of me. I felt like I'd slept with some powerful, beautiful woman who'd taken me whole, and then left me without the will to move, without the will to even roll over, all gone. But I stood up anyway, because god damn it, I still wanted that horn.

The way I was then, there was no use trying to jump old Lucky for his axe. I didn't have the strength to raise my arms, much less grab the old man and run off with his horn.

"Get your shit together, Benny," he said, and pointed over at my tenor in its case. "Go on. Pick up your horn, kid."

I shuffled over to the case and, somehow, I picked it up. It dangled from my arm like a broken limb. I pocketed my mouthpiece and looked back at him; he was still holding that wonderful instrument lightly in his hands.

Lucky let go of the horn with one hand, and held it there in place. He reached back into the pocket of his dark striped suit and pulled out something. "I'm going to give you this, kid." Whatever he pulled out was wrapped in a white handkerchief. "Then I want you to get your ass outa here," he said. "Got it?"

I nodded. Behind me I heard the rats scuffling around in the walls again.

"Yours," Lucky said, and tossed it to me, handkerchief and all.

I dropped the tenor and it crashed on the floor in its case. That sent the rats in the walls rustling into an uproar. But I caught what he tossed to me.

I opened the silk handkerchief and found a glass tube there. It was like the glass casing that comes around expensive cigars. But something dark was stuck inside it, obscured by the dust and oil that comes from frequent handling.

"Junk?" I said, thinking he'd tossed me some kind of drug I didn't know.

"Get out," he yelled.

"I don't do junk anymore," I said.

"Out," he yelled again, and his eyes had turned into a ferocious glare. He seemed to be stronger, and younger suddenly. He seemed to have more heft to him, to suddenly fill out that suit. He smiled again at something. His sallow face seemed to fill with vigor, and he seemed to stand even taller than his six feet. His free hand drifted back to the sax he still held ready, like it was filled to bursting with hot air.

"This is all?" I said, and pocketed the vial.

"Go," he whispered now. The rats scurried and then stopped. Everyone seemed to be waiting. Lucky seemed relaxed.

"All right, man," I said, and hefted my tenor case up again.

As I opened the door, he stood with his back to me, with the sax still poised. "And don't come back here crying to me," he said, without even a glance over his shoulder.

"I just. . . "

"Out," he said.

When I closed the door and it latched itself behind me, I heard him begin to play. That was a beautiful horn, man, rich and fat and warm in tone. But his playing was nothing special, you know. It was just some noodling around on "Caravan," nothing special at all. Not anymore, I guess.

Out in the rainy street I thought about tossing the vial away, man. I didn't really want to get caught carrying around some sort of dope I didn't understand. Not with my record, you know?

But I didn't toss it. I kept it, out of curiosity, I suppose. Things'd been different, you know, if I weren't so damn curious.

I took the thing home to my one room in the Central District, and that night I pulled out the glass tube and tried to figure it out.

I took the silk handkerchief and dampened it, and then used it to polish the crud off the vial. Some of that old dirt I had to scrape loose with a fingernail, and it still wouldn't clean entirely.

It was getting late, like one or two in the morning. So I couldn't quite believe what I found, or what I thought I saw in that vial. As the glass came clean, what was rattling around in that corked tube spooked me. I rubbed my eyes, and then wiped the tube off again. I held it up to the lamp and shook the vial a little. It looked like a finger was stuffed in there.

But I couldn't believe that, man. I cut the old duct tape from around the end of the tube and pried the rubber cork out of it. Immediately the whole room smelled like an old, sweet and sour fart had been set free. Disgusting, man. I spilled the contents out on the table and there it was: a finger. Just like I thought.

The blood on the end was all dried black and rusted, but other than that the finger looked just fine. It wasn't decomposed at all, and it hadn't shriveled. The tube, I suppose, kept it from curling up. It was a short, plump, right little finger. And it was black. Lucky had given me some black cat's right pinky. And it scared the hell out of me.

I scooped the thing back into the vial without touching it, using the rubber cork as a prod. Then I corked the tube up tight again. I wrapped the vial back up in the wet, dirty hanky, and I noticed then the monogram woven in the silk: ELT, with the L as the big middle letter.

I shoved the whole thing in a bottom drawer of my dresser. Then I wondered if I'd been made a party to some kind of murder or something. I remembered some of the cats I used to borrow from to get stuff, and how they were prone to breaking little things like toes and fingers when they weren't happy. Now I've been clean for two years, but it got me to wondering about old debts I could have forgotten. That sent me in a couple bounds across the room to the door. I locked it up tight, man, and shoved the old couch in front of it. Then I switched out the lights.

I pulled down the Murphy bed, and I climbed in it. Yeah, I pulled the covers up over my head like a kid, and I hid there until I fell asleep. Music was the farthest thing from my mind, you know. I was scared goofy.

Before the first light I woke with a start. I sat up straight in the bed and knew what it was. I went through the list of names in my head and counted them, and it was right. There were nine of them. He'd run through nine names while I blew my little take on the "Yardbird Suite." Lucky was the tenth. He finished the set.

Gray dawn was working through the fog, and I went over to the drawer and opened it and got Lucky's handkerchief out. I unveiled the tube gently on the dresser top. Suddenly all that old fruit's talk about saints and relics and trail rides with dead bodies made sense. He'd given me a relic, man. A sacred, magic relic.

And if it was true, and it made me a part of that list of names he'd rattled off, then it was time for me to find out what I could do.

I wrapped the vial back up and put it gently in my pants pocket. I got my tenor out, set the reed and I blew. Normally, at an hour like this, at dawn here, I wouldn't even think of playing. Not even with some kind of mute in the horn. I had neighbors all around me, up, down, on both sides. They'd most likely call the cops if I ever tried to play at dawn.

But not this morning, man. Because suddenly I had that spark Lucky was talking about. I blew softly at first, but that didn't last long. See, I was lifted up into the music, you know, playing no tune at all, but all with such simple beauty and invention, no one complained. Nobody, man. There was no yelling, no feet stomped on the floor, no pounding on the walls, no phone calls to the police or to the building super. Everybody, including me, we all just listened, stunned by the beauty laid bare in the fog and the dawn.

I'd never played like that before. I'd rarely even heard anything like it before. But then, I never had the hands of the Bird in my hip pocket before.

Two

Within the first week, Ching found me. Everything happened fast then, once I was with her. When I think back on it, I can't believe how fast your whole life can change on you, when you've got that spark.

For the first two or three days, I didn't go out at all. I'm not even sure how long I spent like that, because I was lost in it, man. I just played and played and played. I didn't stop to eat . I just drank down some water every now and then to help keep the reeds wet, and I played and played and then played some more. I couldn't believe it myself. After a time, I'd be so exhausted from blowing that I'd collapse back on the bed and sleep. When I came to, with just a drink of water I'd be back to that horn. Day, night, whatever, it didn't matter, man. I was lost in this enormous land of discovery, and I didn't care if I fell off the edge of the world, because I had to know what else I could say. What more could I find in that old horn?

I lost some days like that--I don't know how many--and then one morning, I came to on the floor in the middle of my room. I knew I was done with it. My lips were dry and cracked from playing.

There was a streak of dried blood running from the corner of my mouth, where my lips had bled. But I hadn't noticed it. My shoulders felt stiff from holding the tenor up so long, and my chest hurt, though I couldn't figure out why. I thought maybe I'd played so much I'd strained my lungs.

But it was all like a ritual then, you know. I moved the couch away from the door and unlocked it. Then I went and took a long warm bath and shaved my face clean. I dressed and put the vial gently in my pocket, packed up the tenor, and strode out the door. That first morning, I found a restaurant and feasted on a breakfast of steak and eggs and lots of juice, until I felt restored.

Then I hopped a bus and walked down to the Market, and I set up there under an awning. I looked at all these people strolling by, ignoring me, and I felt happy. I planted my feet wide and I leaned back and played. It took a little while, because at first no one listened. But before very long a crowd started to gather, you know. Somehow I knew it would. It grew bigger and bigger, until I couldn't even see all those faces out there. I just heard people shushing at one another.

Nobody applauded or said much, and not a single one of them tossed even a coin in my case. But I didn't care, man. I wasn't doing this for money now. They were all too surprised, I think. They just stood and listened and didn't even look at me. When I'd pause, I'd hear a lot of them breathe, man, so I think some of them were holding their breath and they didn't even know it. It was like the music I played had become their breathing.

After an hour or so, I was tired and my lip had started to bleed again, so I stopped. But the people still hung around, and didn't seem to know what to do or say. I packed up and looked out at the faces and just said, "Tomorrow, man." Then I left. I went straight home and slept until dawn the next day, I think.

Then I did it all again. The unlocking, the long bath, the big feast for strength, and then down to the street again to play. As I grew stronger, and my lips calloused with the playing and my shoulders and chest strengthened, I blew longer and longer. The crowds got bigger and stayed as long as I could stand to play. I always left them crowded together and speechless at the end. There was nothing to say. Words were shot, man. The world was divided, you know, into just music, and then the end of music. And I was the one who stood in the middle, I chose which way the street would go.

About the third day after that, it was time to see if this was real. I mean, I'd been playing in the Market for a bunch of tourists, you know. They were there hoping to be distracted. I was working an easy crowd when you got right down it. Even if my playing did blow them away, what did that show? They were looking for something to get blasted on.

The real test was uptown, man. Where the folk were working. I planted myself up on Fifth in the shadow of the big banks, and I didn't start until it was a little after one in the afternoon. For a while I just watched all these suits rushing by, scurrying around making money. They were so in intent, you know, they were funny. If I could enchant this crowd, then I knew what I had in my pocket was as full of magic as I believed it was.

And you know, it didn't take long. They were easy. I just dove into a slow, mournful "You Don't Know What Love Is," and they were easier than cheap whores. Man, those suits were hungry for what they were missing. It surprised the hell out of me. They stopped right where they were walking, and then those suits piled up like a log jam in a flooded river. Before I drove on through a third chorus and then left the changes behind, they were overflowing out into the street and stopping cars. I had dammed up a nice little lake of gray suits, men and women both, dressed like a million dollars and standing in the drizzle, listening as their time and their money drifted by riding along on my reed. I ended up with a couple cops out there, too. They probably came on a call to clear the traffic, but they were as flat-footed as the straight cats in suits beside them. I had them all, man. Hip pocket, babe. In there. Mine.

That was when Ching found me. After I stopped and grinned out at the stunned crowd, she was the first one to move. She slipped her way up through that gaggle of gray suits. Once she moved and broke the spell, I heard the cops coming to and suddenly yelling out orders. "Lets move it along now. Outa da street, folks." Ellen Ching walked toward me though, and the crowd let her move through because she was so tall, and so beautiful.

She wore a grin at just one corner of her mouth, but as she walked up to me, it broadened into a full smile. It wrinkled up her eyes and showed her small teeth so white they startled. She was wearing black boots with three inch heels, but she was an easy six foot without them. She sauntered right up to me, put a hand gently on my shoulder, and said, "You play like an angel, honey. Where you been hiding?"

I grinned back at her and bent down to lay my tenor in its case. Then I shrugged and said, "Around."

Now, I've been with a few women; what cat who can play even half assed hasn't? I know how to talk to a lady, you know. But she was different, man. I didn't know what to say to her.

"I'm Ellen Ching," she said and stuck out her hand. "Friends call me Ching."

I shook her hand, then I said my name.

She nodded her head as if she was putting that on file. Her eyes were dark and her color was a rich, olive brown. She was dressed all in black and in leather, except for a silk scarf--it was stoplight red--draped around her shoulders. Her black hair was clipped short and it was as unruly as a boy's, and on one side there was a streak of cobalt blue dyed into it. She wore a plain silver ring in one ear, and when she'd tilt her head a certain way, it'd reflect a touch of that blue in her hair. Two black leather bands were at her wrists.

"Come with me, Benny Crisp," she said, looking down at me from her height.

It occurred to me, as I followed her down the Ave with my gig bag over my shoulder, she sounded a lot like old Lucky T. I was getting good at following orders. But this was different, you know? Because if she wanted to haul me off into to some dark warehouse and then jump me, baby, I was all hers. She could have the horn, man, as long as she took me with it.

But not Lucky`s vial. Maybe not the vial.

Her behind moved nice in those tight leather pants, and I tagged along with my horn. She never looked back, but she didn't have to, because she knew I was following. And the way she moved in those heels, she most likely had led a few men down the street of dreams like this. I didn't mind. Men and women both were turning to watch her strut past on the sidewalk. You know, she was to the eyes what my music had suddenly become to the ears. Distracting, man. Sliding close to obsession.

At the entrance to one of the big hotels downtown, she looked back, flashed that smile at me like a beacon, and then held open the heavy glass door for me. "Benny," she said, "you and me, we are going places."

I wanted to say something cool, like "Wherever you say, baby, the ticket's on me." But instead I just grinned back and nodded like a kid on his first date.

"You got to be heard, Benny," she said, Sounding as serious as all those money guys I'd stopped in the street. She was leading me across the lobby to an elevator. "And this is not the place. Not here, Benny."

She pulled a key out of somewhere, maybe the scarf, because it wasn't anywhere in all that tight leather or I'd have seen it and been able to read the number. Ching used that key in the elevator controls, and then pushed a button that rode us up to the very top floors of the hotel, past where the numbered buttons on the panel ran.

The elevator opened on a wide, empty hall, speckled with ferns and feathery plants. She strode down it, her sharp heels silent in the plush carpet. The same key opened the door to a broad room, covered with skylights. She tossed the key on the round bed, then looked at herself in the mirror. I stood in the open doorway. She glanced at me out of the mirror, and said, "Come in, come in. Shut the door behind you, Benny."

When I was inside, she stopped and looked me up and down. "You don't know what I can do for you, Benny Crisp," she said. But I had a few ideas.

She touched one bright red nail to her lip, and her other hand ran through her hair and ruffled that short blue streak. "We'll have to do something with the way you look though," she said, frowning.

"But first," she nodded to herself, and the frown stayed in place, "Let's see if I was right." She stepped over to an oak night table by the bed and poured herself a brandy or something in a snifter. When she leaned over to pour from the heavy bottle on the table that was low for her height, the sleek lines in her leather made my mouth go dry in anticipation. "Take out that horn of yours, Benny, and let me hear you play again. Just like you did in the street."

If I'd been Mr. Cool as usual around the ladies, I'd have made a smart crack about what she meant by "Horn." But I wasn't Mr. Cool, man. I was King of the Jerks right then

She slipped off that red scarf and popped those a wrist bands off, tossing them all on the bed near the key. "Let's go outside," she said then. She flashed me her smile and she knew how much it was worth, too. While I took the tenor out and put it together on the floor, she opened some glass doors and strolled out onto a covered parapet. She loosened the top couple buttons of her leather top and then the silk blouse beneath it. As I followed her outside, she took a sip and slipped herself into a low slung lounger. Her long legs were crossed and dangling over the arms.

It took me a while to wet the reed again. Ellen Ching just smiled, and sipped, and waited without another word.

This time I started, awkwardly, with an old tune. I'd worn this song down to a smooth shine, man, playing it out on the street in the old days. Before I had the charm in my pocket. But it was the only thing that came into my rattled head then, you know? "Someone to Watch Over Me." She laughed when she caught the melody. Then she took a drink. It was all pretty lame, and Ellen Ching looked pretty worried at first.

But then, finally, the vial in my pocket took over, you know. It started by adding just a few blue notes and growls to the melody. But before long it lead me away from the chords and back into that world of pure melody where it liked to live on purified air and thin beaten gold. "Someone" disappeared and the hands of Bird watched over me, man. They played my dreams and touched on everybody's. Ching set her drink on the floor, and then, later, started to cry without making a sound. I was afraid to stop playing, because I wouldn't know what to say.

"That's beautiful, Benny," she said, when my shoulders and arms started to ache enough they made me quit. "Where did you learn to play like that? I've never heard anything even close to it? It's as if you're playing inside me, Benny, playing what my heart has always wanted to hear."

I should have told her then about the relic. It was the only answer there was to her question. But I was afraid, man. And I was weak. If I told her it was the vial, man, she'd want it and not me. She wouldn't love me. And she'd take that little relic, because I'd give it to her if she asked, and she'd leave me alone again.

But if I kept it a secret, I could have her. And that seemed like all I needed just then.

"Thank you, Lucky," I muttered.

"Oh, that's more than luck, Benny," Ching said. "You've got something special there."

She stood and strode back inside and picked up the phone. I took out that vial full of magic and used Lucky 's handkerchief to staunch the bleeding that had started again on my lip. Then I unwrapped it enough to see the gray nail on that finger inside the glass. Ching was talking to someone inside.

"Michael, Michael," she said, loud enough so I could hear it clearly. "Believe me," she said.

When I bent down and carefully packed the horn away, she was talking to someone else, someone called Rudy now. I carefully fit the vial in the case, in the slot where the mouthpiece was meant to rest. It fit snug and safe, especially when I settled the Otto Link on top of it.

By the time I walked back in the room, she said, "Set it all up with Michael, will you, Rudy? Just trust me. You're going to love this."

Next it was to the airlines, and she was making two reservations on a morning flight for La Guardia. I looked down at my horn case, thinking about where that little vial was stored. "Three," I said.

With a pause, Ching winked at me and told them to make it three seats, and had them deliver the tickets to the hotel. She called down and told the desk she'd be checking out in the morning and to send the plane tickets up when they came.

"That third seat," she laid the phone back in its cradle. "It is for your horn, isn't it?" Her smile sparkled again.

I nodded yes and all she said was, "Good."

The rain cleared off and the clouds broke up that afternoon, like it never does here. Ching hauled me around then, and dressed me. We bought three suits and then what she called my "stage attire." This was a pure white painter's smock that hung to my knees, pants and shoes as rich and red as blood, and a small black beret that she hung off the back of my head. "We'll save this for your debut," she said, as she adjusted it on my head. The suits were all black and conservative and pricey, and I bought a nice little pork-pie hat like the Prez to go with them. The one last suit was pin-striped, and when I wore it I felt like Lucky T. Ching wasn't too wild about it, but I insisted. And so I got my Lucky suit.

All of this was a long way from playing in the street.

When we were done with the haberdasheries and the tailors we went back to her hotel room in the sky. She ordered up salmon grilled over mesquite from room service, and a lot of wine I couldn't even pronounce. We ate and silently watched the snow on Mt. Rainier change from gold to pink, and then to rose as the sun set behind the

Olympics. She held up a glass of blushing wine in the last faint light, and toasted us. "To the next giant step," she said. As we drank, I thought about whether she meant the music or the promotion. It was a moonless night, and we were far up above the city lights. It was totally dark in Ching's room, so the skylights filled with black space and flickering stars. And after dinner, on the big round bed, Ching took off her black vest and her long black boots. Underneath all the leather and silk, there was nothing but more stars and the endless heavens.

On the plane the next morning, she sat beside me, and the horn, with its little secret, was on my other side. I was in love. I sat between the most beautiful woman I'd ever known and the most beautiful music I'll ever hear. And they both were mine for the taking.

"Can you do it again?" Ching said. "In the street?" There was a frown of concern that wrinkled her eyes, as if she was afraid of losing me.

"The street?" I said, a little confused until I realized she meant my playing.

Her bright smile flashed back then, and she said, "Of course, you can. You were stopping the streets in Seattle. Wait until they hear you in New York."

I just nodded my head, then I reached out and laid a hand on her bare knee. "I got my music," I said. She was wearing a red dress that clung to her the same way I wanted to.

Ching let her head fall back as she laughed. That blue streak in her black hair made the sky out the plane window seem pale. She put her hand over mine on her knee and held it there. "My, My," she laughed, "aren't we growing confident." I smiled at her. Then she leaned across the seat and kissed my ear, licking it.

"Hey," I said, and pulled back.

"That's good, Benny, that's good," she said, laughing at me. The flight attendant came up, looking at where my hand was resting. She set our drinks down, and smiled through her teeth at us.

"You're gonna need that confidence in the Big Apple," Ching said.

Three

We made love on the carpet in her apartment, in a bay window that looked down on Washington Square. It was noon, and people were eating lunch out there as the leaves fell around them on the concrete. I was wrapped up in Ching's long, olive legs, and her red dress was beside us on the rug. All she wore was her one earring and her leather wristbands. My headed rested on her chest, between her breasts, and I listened to the rhythm of her hard breathing, and I heard the swing of my horn in her heart.

"I want you to play down in the Square," she said, between her breaths. It seemed like I heard the words inside of her. "Just like you did back there. Just blow them all into oblivion, Benny, like you did back there. When Michael gets here."

"Michael?" I said and lifted my head. She was smiling at me.

"He's a record producer," Ching kissed my brow. "He's going to do a lot for you, Benny. Once he hears you." She looked up at the ceiling, and I watched the perfect lines of her dark eyes.

"Wait 'til he hears you," she said.

"When does he get here?" I said, leaning up and biting the point of her chin.

She laughed. Then she said, "Anytime now."

"What?" I said.

I rolled free of her long thighs and her flat stomach, where our sweat had held us together. I looked down at the people lunching in the Village. "Maybe we should get dressed," I said.

"Oh, Benny," she tapped my cheek with her fingers. "Maybe we should."

She stood up and walked away from me, and I still couldn't believe her beautiful round behind. I picked up her dress and my pants and followed her. But she was leaning down, at a mirror, ruffling that blue streak in her hair. A knock came at the door.

"Just a minute, Michael, dear," she said, loud enough to be heard out in the hall. "Could you get that for me, Benny?" she said.

"Ching?" a man's voice said out in the hall.

I was hopping around trying to get my pants back on, not even close to putting on a shirt. "Be right there," I yelled.

"Ain't got all day, people," another voice said, deeper and raspy.

"What the hell?" I muttered and stumbled over to lean on a wall to pull my suit pants up. "You invite the whole damn record company, or something?"

Ching had slipped a red silk robe around her that reached to the floor. "Rudy? Is that you?" she said. Then she strolled right past me, only pausing to pat me once on the butt. Suddenly, I felt like a race horse.

The knock rattled the door again. "Coming," she said. "Coming, gentlemen."

I had my shirt on and tucked in, but only half buttoned up, when Ching opened the door and let these two guys in: a tall, reddish blonde cat in a big blousy white shirt wearing a brown leather vest, and a little guy, thick and hunched over like he'd been a wrestler in high school, and wearing a sweatshirt with the sleeves pulled over his forearms. She hugged them both and the tall guy kissed her on the cheek.

These two guys looked nervous and strung out to me. The tall cat in the vest shuffled his feet a lot on the carpet, and neither of them ever stood still.

"Benny, this is Michael Browning," Ching put her hand on the tall guy's shoulder. He nodded a lot, quickly, then he pulled on the droopy end of his big blonde mustache.

"And this is Rudy," she said, and put her arm around the little wrestler. He was bald, and she planted a big kiss on his head. "Better known as Otto Rudio," she said then

"Rudio," I said.

Ching grinned when I knew the name. "Best engineer in the record business, Benny."

Rudio just nodded his head at me.

"And Michael?" Ching strolled over and wrapped her arms around my waist, "Rudy? This is you're next big project." I was still buttoning my shirt. She fluffed at my hair little. "This is," Ching paused there and thought a moment. Then she turned on that big smile. "This is the Dove," she said. And that was where the name came from.

"So, kid," Michael Browning said, though he was about the same age as me. "What you got to show us?" He tugged again at his mustache.

"Benny, get dressed," Ching stroked my hair back and straightened it then. "I'll deal with Michael and Rudy."

They sent me out in the street to prove myself, you know. I was wearing my Lucky suit, with all his gray chalk stripes, and my pork pie hat, and toting my horn. I could see the three of them up above the square, looking out Ching's bay window, watching me.

I got to admit, man, it was brilliant of her. I was used to the street, you know. I'd played outside for years. Ching knew that, and she'd seen what I could do out there. So she used it, man, she played to my strengths.

I walked over near the arch in the Square. A couple guys with a blaster were going after some kind of rap, but nobody was paying them much attention. It was a nice fall afternoon in New York, and people were carrying their jackets and strolled by, taking their time. At least, as much as New Yorkers can take their time. I got my horn out, and put the vial gently in my suit pocket. Nobody paid any attention to me, you know.

How many saxophones had they heard in Washington Square over the years? How many street musicians had offered their wares out here? I was just another two bit axe, with my heart out on the street, asking for two dollar bills. But I was used to that, man. A boom box is just a new variation on the old accordion and tuba crowd. It was time for me to blow the competition away.

I planted my feet and looked up to Ching and her two friends. I noticed then she had the windows open. When I set the reed and was ready, she blew me a big kiss I could see all the way across the street.

At first, I just played into that beating blaster's groove. The rappers kept on, even trading a riff or two with me. It was all one pretty old set of tricks, you know?

I saw Browning the tall guy walk away from the window. Ching looked over her shoulder and said something to him. Rudio just stood, listening, his thick arms hanging at his sides like he was ready to wrestle me to the ground. Ching waved an arm at me, urging me on.

That was when I felt the vial take over. The horn began to play out of the beat, first just a little behind the blaster's heavy groove, and then into rhythm just a little ahead of it. The notes started to come in triplets on every beat, and then I started to growl and wail, and the rules of that rap seemed to die away.

I saw Michael come back to the window, beside Rudy. The little guy's head started to bounce and Michael let go of his mustache long enough to cross his arms on his chest. Ching's shining smile came on, and that made me happiest of all. Then I closed my eyes and was gone into black, solid sound.

When I opened my eyes again, the window was a empty. Washington Square was full. Taxis were stopped in the street, but there weren't any horns honking. Nobody in Greenwich Village had the meter running.

Now Rudio couldn't sit still. He just kept walking around Ching's apartment, shaking his head, and saying, " Benny, Benny, Benny," over and over again.

Michael Browning was sitting on the love seat, but his feet were still shuffling on the carpet. Both of those cats forgot entirely about all the important places they had to be just moments before. "We got to do this right," Michael was saying. "This is important shit, Rudy."

Ching was stretched out on the carpet near those bay windows. She was smiling regally. One long leg had slipped free of the red robe, and it was smooth and olive brown and ended in forever.

"Benny, Benny, Benny," Rudy goes.

"This is gonna make some big noise, Ching," Michael Browning kept talking, to himself really. "If we spring him right."

"I want to get him live, Michael. Such energy, you know? It's got to be live. But not outside, man." Rudy kept pointing a finger at Michael.

I bent down and put the vial back in its safe little notch in my case. Then I took off my Lucky jacket.

"Where'd you learn to play that way?" Ching said to me again.

"We may not get that energy, Michael, in a studio," Rudy was smacking a fist in his open hand now.

I went into the kitchen and opened up Ching's refrigerator, hoping to find a beer. There was a lot of spring water and fruit in there, man, and that's it. But I was dying of thirst. So I grabbed one of those little green bottles of water and popped it open.

"The Dove, yeah, I like that," Michael got up and started to pace. "Great idea, Ching. The Dove. Perfect. Perfect," he says.

I took a long swig of the nothing in that water bottle. I looked back in the room and Ching was watching me. She wore that big smile, and she winked at me. Then she pulled her robe around her long legs and stood up.

"There was the Hawk. And the Bird. Now comes," Michael thrust his hands up to square off the marquee in his imagination. "The Dove," he said. Then he nodded, "I like it."

Ching sauntered into the kitchen, stroked my check gently, and then opened a cabinet. It was filled with bottles. "What would you like?" she said.

"A beer, Ching."

"Benny, Benny," she shook her head at me like a school teacher. But none of my teachers ever wore red silk robes and blue streaked hair, you know. At least not while they were around me. "Benny, you're background is showing."

She reached over and opened a drawer there in the kitchen cupboard, pulled out a leather bank bag, unzipped it and extracted one bill. It all went back in the bottom drawer, and she handed the bill to Michael.

"Go get some beer, Michael. Your 'Dove' is thirsty," she said.

"The Vanguard," Rudy said. "That's where I want to record him. That's the perfect room for live cuts." He was nodding his head. "Call Max," he said, looking over at Michael.

I was sipping my beer, and nearly choked on the word. "The Village Vanguard?" I said. Shit, the Vanguard, man.

But then I started thinking about really playing there, and about all the great ones who'd made a record there. Rollins, 'Trane, Dexter, you know? I went down the line, and realized then we were talking about all ten fingers, man. The Hands of the Bird. "Yeah," I said. "Why not?" I said. I was feeling like I ought to take my place there. I was part of it now. The Hands.

"Max'll be tough," Michael said.

"Call him," Rudy said, and looked like he'd take Mr. Browning and wrestle him into a knot, if he didn't get this done right.

"We'll record him two nights," Rudy says. "On night to get the levels and let Benny get used to the room and the crowd, you know. A rehearsal.

And the next night for posterity, man. The next night is the killer?"

Ching smiled and took a sip of her bottled water. She was still wearing the red silk robe and nothing else, and she was sitting on the arm of the chair I was sitting in, with her hand resting on my shoulder. "A premiere, Michael," she said. "We'll fill the room with all the right people. Musicians, critics, you know. Everybody who counts. A Monday night, when everybody's free. And Rudy will make a record of the night New York first heard the Dove."

Michael's feet started shuffling on the carpet again. "I like it," his head was nodding and the mustache was getting a workout. "It's like being there to record on the first night Ornette played in New York, or like opening night with the '39 Basie band. Yeah. I like it. Live at the Vanguard, the Apple meets the Dove. It's perfect, man."

"Call Max," Rudy goes, still looking like he meant it.

"Benny," Michael stood up, shuffled his feet some more, and looked at me. "You just do what you did out there, and were gonna put you on the cover of every magazine from *downbeat* to *Wire*. The Big Apple Meets the Dove."

"What's wrong with the cover of *Time*?" Ching patted my shoulder.

"Make the call, Michael," Rudy says, and smacked his fist again.

I sat up in bed, not knowing where I was, and couldn't breathe. I gasped at the air and it seemed to catch in the bottom of my throat, and it couldn't get any further. Everything was dark in the room, and I grabbed my neck. I pulled at it, like maybe I could rip it open and let the air in, you know. But all I could do was roar once and let all the air in me out.

Ching, somehow, shoved me out of bed and onto the floor. She kneeled on my back and beat on it with both her fists. It seemed to take all of time, all the time there was in this universe, and I was still squeezing my throat like it was a rope I was clinging to, but eventually I began to cough. I spat out mucous and blood and food, and then slowly, twisting flat on the floor, I began to get air.   It began to come back in, and it was like I was rising out of some closed in place.

"Slow, baby, slow," Ching pleaded in my ear. She lay on my back and seemed to help pump the air into me with her weight.

In a while we were stretched out on the floor next to one another. And that's when we started to laugh. I mean, what else could you do, you know? I was laughing because I felt like some kind of an idiot. And I guess I was laughing because I could just plain breathe again, because it was a false alarm. Maybe that was why Ching was laughing, too, you know. It was relief, man.

The whole deal, from choking to death all the way to laughing to death on that floor, took maybe ten minutes, tops. But it seemed like a year, you know. Maybe a year and a half.

"Last time I let you drink that much beer," Ching said.

I was coming around enough to realize we were both lying on the floor naked. She got up and came back with a couple of warm, damp towels and a little green bottle of that fancy water.

"Last time I eat so much Chinese food," I said at her, and grinned.

See, after we'd gotten rid of Michael and Rudy, Ching had cooked for me. Then we ate and drank beer and talked about all the things we were going to do together, until we were full, and then went off to make love in her feather bed. The one I'd just fallen out of.

We cleaned up the mess of blood and crap I'd made on the floor, and on both of our bodies. Strange as it may seem, mopping it all up with towels seemed to excite us. I never thought so much sweat and blood could be a turn on but I was wrong. Maybe it was just the relief though, you know. I was still giddy just to be alive.

But before long I was making love to Ching again in on the floor. The breathing came easy.

Still, that was the night it happened the first time, I'm sure. It was right about then. And we thought it was just a stupid, scary accident. Then.

*

A lot of what I'd call "music business shit" ate up the next week or two. There was the problem of who was going to accompany me, most of all. See, I wanted to play solo, but Michael and Ching thought that was a mistake. It was too sparse, and it left me too bare up there for a big premiere. This was gonna be a club date, man. I was not playing the streets any more. I had to be a pro about it.

So a string of piano players and bass players and a couple drummers passed through a rehearsal space in a warehouse on the Lower East Side. I played with them all, and in every setting, man, I sounded good. They were some good cats, those players, and some of them were names, too, but I won't mention anybody. Because in the end, I'd always lose them. They could only follow me to a certain point, and then my music would leave them far behind. And what was worse, in trying to play as group, they'd wind up holding me back. So we'd send the duo or trio behind me away, scratching their heads, and then Ching and Michael and I would argue about what to do.

I begged them to let me play it alone, because whatever arrangement you set me in, I was limited by it. Whoever it was, at least until I figured this music out myself, it was holding me back. I needed to go it alone, for a time. I needed to let the rest of the music catch up with me.

It took days and days of auditions before I convinced them, first Ching and then slowly Michael Browning. I needed to play the gig alone. Finally, they gave in. I think, in the end, Ching even saw it my way.   I had to play solo, until the world caught up with what I was doing with that vial.

Convincing Max was another story.

"In the morning!" Max's voice on the phone was loud enough I could hear it clear across the room.

Ching wanted to stage another street scene for Max's benefit, another little spontaneous concert in Washington Square. But Michael shot that down, right out of the air, man. Suddenly it was important to keep me a secret. I was going to be a major surprise for old Manhattan. "We want to cause a sensation," Michael kept saying. A surprise attack on the ears of the City. Just me and my horn. Already word was leaking out, through all those cats we auditioned. On the street there was talk that something new was here, and the players better be ready. A change was gonna come. And Michael wanted this Vanguard guard gig to cause that change, all at once. "A shock wave, Ching," he said. "That's what we're after."

So there was no more street playing, man. My days of that were over, he said.

"That's right, Max," Michael said into Ching's phone. "Tomorrow morning. We don't want anybody but you at the club, my man. We're keeping this one under wraps, Max." Michael paused and listened a moment, nodded his head. "That's right, Rudy and I want to hear him in the room first. And trust me, Max, you want to hear him in your room."

I guess the rumblings about me had reached as far as Mr. Max, because he agreed. On a Sunday morning, I warmed up my horn with some riffs and scales, then Ching and I taxied over to the Vanguard. Michael and Rudy were waiting for us in the basement, along with the owner. Max was about four feet tall, with hair as white and shining as Ching's smile.

"No rhythm section?" Max said, when he saw me alone up there, putting together my horn. I slipped Lucky's handkerchief and the vial out, put it in my jeans pocket.

"But nobody's played horn solo at the Vanguard," Max said, looking out at Michael like he was nuts. Rudy was wandering around the back of the room already, thinking about microphones and placement. "Even Sonny played with a trio," Max complained, shaking his head.

Michael put his arm around the little guy's shoulders. "Trust me," he said, tugging at his drooping mustache with his free hand. "You're gonna love it, Max."

I looked around the room, from up on the small stage, and I saw the walls full of photographs of heroes of mine, every one of them standing up here, playing on this same little stage. Monk and 'Trane, Mingus, and Dexter. Everybody, man, everybody was there.

I looked across the room, and on the back wall I saw a familiar face. It was all the way across the barroom, and I never did get up close to check it out, but it was him. I didn't need to check it out. It was Lucky wailing away on that alto, way in the back where Ching was poking around, waiting for me to play. It was Lucky. And now I could feel it, way out there on them bricks, baby, my picture was going up the wall, too. Hands of the Bird, baby. Lucky.

I patted the vial in my pocket, then I played, slowly, a simple blues scale up the horn in B flat. You know I sounded like an old master of the horn, just my big warm tone speaking years and years of the blues, and just riding on a simple scale. Then my fingers took off from there, you know, and I blew hard and deep for almost an hour. No one--except Ching who was already on the inside of my magic--no one but Ching moved during that whole hour. Mr. Rudy stopped and stood still and forgot all about his mikes and angles. Mr. Michael stopped tugging on that poor 'stache. And Max shut up.

Ching strolled toward me from under Lucky's picture and sat on the stage at my feet. That's when she noticed the shape of that little vial in the pocket of my jeans.

When I was done, she whispered at me, "What's in your pocket, Benny?"

I laid the horn down in the case, and Max was nodding his head up and down, talking with Michael about moving dates around, giving the Monday Night Orchestra a rest, making room for my big two night premiere. "And then I want the Dove back in here for two weeks straight," he was saying, "as soon as we can open up a couple weeks for him." He stood up and started wandering around, looking for a calendar, while he held an appointment book in his hand.

"You ain't got the monkey on your back, do you, Benny?" Ching touched the pocket of my jeans with her fingers. I took out the vial carefully, and tucked it back in its safe place.

"No, baby," I said. That's when the pain in my chest brightened and I started to cough again. "Later," I said. I couldn't get another word out.

"This room is right," Rudy said from the back of the room by the bar. "I got it." Then, "Perfect, Benny," he goes, "perfect."

"Remember, we want the marquee empty, Max. These first two nights are invitation only," Michael was going on. "No signs in the window."

"Benny?" Ching said, because she saw it coming over me again.

I didn't hear much more, because she ushered me down the narrow hall, under the stairs, to the bathroom, where I coughed and spat up blood for fifteen minutes.

"You're not doing some sort of junk, are you?" she said.

I was sipping that fancy bottled water and lounging on her bed with my shirt off. I shook my head no.

"'Cause if you are, Mr. Benny Crisp, you can find your way to the door." Her narrow eyes were darker than usual, filled with some old hurt. "I've had enough of you musicians and your junk."

"I'm clean, Miss Ellen, ma'am," I grinned. She was lying on her stomach near me on the bed. She was wearing jeans and a white sleeveless T-shirt. Plain attire for her, man, but she'd still stop me in the street by just strolling past. I touched the cobalt blue in her black hair and let my finger play through it.

Her smile came on and she bit at my hand. She laughed and climbed on top of me. "So what was that you had in your pocket, Benny? What do you keep hiding so carefully in that case of yours."

I told her then about Lucky and the warehouse, about the rainy night and the relic he gave me, about the way I used to play and the way I play now, and about the nine other fingers and what was in that little vial. About the Bird. I even wondered out loud whether it had something to do with the way I couldn't breathe that morning.

Ching pushed off my shoulders and fell back the bed, laughing at me. "Baby, there ain't no relic can do what you are doing with that horn."

"You don't believe me?" I said, leaning over to her, grinning down, wanting her again.

"Oh, I believe you, Benny," she said. "I believe you're nuts."

I pulled her T-shirt up then and tickled the muscles on her brown stomach with my tongue. She laughed and said through her laughter, "You play one bitching horn though, Benny boy." That's when she pulled the rest of my clothes off.   I remember that.

I woke up later that night, because the bed was empty. For a moment I was afraid I couldn't breathe. I panicked at first and sat up, but I was all right, and it took only a moment's breath to know. But Ching was crouched over on the floor, naked, fooling around in my case.   She had Lucky's handkerchief in her hand, and I could see my blood on it, a dark stain, even across the room at night. It came at me like a pouncing cat or something, you know. I was afraid again.

"Be careful with that," I said.

"You are weird, Benny Crisp," she said.

"Come back to bed."

She smiled and her eyes wrinkled closed. "Weird is such a turn on," she laughed, and crawled back on all fours to the bed.

She was right.

Two weeks before opening night, and I had nothing but a lot of time to kill. I listened to reels and reels of studio tapes at Michael Browning's apartment and over in New Jersey at Rudy's studio. Once Ching and I rented a car and drove out to Montauk, we rode the ferry to Staten Island and rented bikes, we rode the trains to Rockaway and to Coney Island, we found strange little restaurants to enjoy. We went to clubs at night--Sweet Basil, The Blue Note, Tonic--and we heard lot of fine music.

Music like I used to play. But nothing close to what I was reaching for now, man.

It was difficult to practice, because Michael was trying to keep me under such tight wraps. It's hard to find a place to play in a crowded city, when you're a secret, man. It wound up I practiced in the Vanguard. Every morning, for the ten days or so before I opened, Ching and I would walk over to the club at dawn and I'd practice for an hour or so. Then we'd have breakfast down the street, and be off to kill the rest of the day.

It was a way to live, you know? Sort of the opposite of being a musician. Up early, create something, and then enjoy the day. And we did, because with Ching every moment as a new delight.

Not once in two weeks did I have any trouble. I just blew and blew that horn in wondrous ways for Ellen Ching, while she listened and glowed in my mind like a neighboring galaxy. I began to forget my fears and my doubts. I began to believe it really was me, and not some vial. Because there never was even a catch in my throat.

When the *Village Voice* appeared that week, an inside story covered a mysterious tenor sax player known only as "the Dove." No one had heard him in public yet, but this Dove cat was raising a lot of fire and wind among the musicians around the Downtown scene. There was even a rumor he had something to do with a traffic tie up around Washington Square a few weeks back. Word on the street had it that Monday night a secret, solo concert, open by invitation only, was going down somewhere in the Village. Maybe even at the Vanguard, which was conveniently closed for renovations on two nights that same week.

Michael was pissed off. The last thing he wanted, he said, was a crowd milling around the Vanguard Monday night. Right when all these musicians and critics were showing up. But those cats who'd backed me during all those auditions, they were talking. What could you do? The word was out, and it might ruin everything on Monday night. That was what had Michael upset enough to shuffle his feet and tug his mustache off.

"I think he leaked the story himself," I said. "He's just acting pissed off to cover his tracks."

Ching kissed me on the forehead and nodded with a smile.

"You did it," I said.

She winked, and patted my cheek. "Secret," she said, touched my lips with the red nail of her index finger, and I laughed.

She dressed me that night. The white smock and the blood red pants and shoes she bought me. She arranged the black beret on my head, then stepped back to admire her work. "The horn," she said, and she listened while I warmed it up. Let's polish it 'til it gleams," she said when I was done, and set to work on it with a soft cloth.

"You're going to make history tonight," she said. "It's your maiden flight."

There is no backdoor when you enter the Vanguard, not as far as Ellen Ching is concerned. About ten o'clock she called a cab and we rode the few blocks over to the club. There was the crowd milling about that Michael had feared. Ching smiled to see them hanging around under the awning. But they didn't know me, and paid me no attention. I was just another big shot slipping into the closed and silent Vanguard. We stepped inside and Ching took my coat. Together we unpacked the horn. We would enter down the stairs from the street right into the crowd. That's the way she wanted it. "You're a street musician, aren't you?" she said.

I heard the soft mumble of conversation as I wound down the dark basement stair into the room. I held the horn, clipped to my strap, ready to play. Ching was in front of me, carrying the case. Just before we could be seen, she turned and handed me the bloody handkerchief that held the vial. "It seems you believe you need this," she smiled. "Did you forget?" Then she kissed me on the cheek.

She stepped down out of the way, back toward the kitchen carrying the empty tenor case, and left me alone. The dim room went quiet as I entered.

I had to walk through a crowd of little tables, and every face at every table was turned to see "The Dove." My mouth went dry as I looked around. The tables were full, and I mean everybody was there. Every player with a rep in the City, and every critic who counted for much, not to mention other people I didn't recognize. But I knew from Michael

Browning they were probably record people. They were all there.

But it was the musicians, you know. These other folks you can bluff, because they're only looking for something they can sell. I could blow them away with a little noise and the cool cat get up Ching had bought for me. But not the musicians, man, not Cecil, not Ornette or Sonny, not Threadgill or Haden. They were there to listen, and maybe to learn, but definitely to find out what this music was about. They were going to hear me, man. I mean hear. You know?

So my mouth was dry as I stepped up on the stage and looked out at them. I saw Rudy flash me the okay, and then lean over his panel in the back like the wrestling match was about to begin. I put the horn to my lips and the room went dead silent, the way a real night club full of ofays never is. I was going to be heard, man, by real ears. I was too dry to start though, and to stall I cleared my throat. A little round of whispered conversation and chuckles went through the crowd, as I stood there trying not to look nervous and failing miserably at it.

Michael Browning's voice came from somewhere, yelling, "Give it to 'em, Dove." That got a laugh out of the antsy crowd.

I saw Ching, leaning on my upright case, and she seemed worried. Then she held her hand near her face, with just her little finger up, and flashed that smile of hers at me.

I nodded to her, and touched the vial in my pocket and remembered: it isn't me. Even if Ellen

Ching didn't believe that, she knew enough to use it. But she's wrong, man. It isn't me. Hands of the Bird, man. Lucky's touch. That old magic spark.

I wondered, then, how many of those cats out there looking on me, how many of them were part of these Hands, you know? Hands of the Bird. How many of them carried a little relic in their cases?

I looked to the back of the room, to Lucky's picture on the wall. But I couldn't see it there. Maybe the room was too dark, maybe Rudy was set up in front of it. But it didn't seem to be there, anymore. Lucky seemed to be gone. It isn't me, I told myself.

I closed my eyes and blew through a chorus of "Lover Man," and the musicians chuckled and settled in to listen. Ice clinked in glasses, and chairs were shuffled around some. You could say they relaxed, and it made them laugh. The familiar meant the safe, and even the way out cats don't like dangling off the edge all the time. Especially when somebody else's new thing is shoving them over it, man.

For the first time, on that one night in the Vanguard, I understood what it was I was playing. I understood where the relic had been taking me all this time. I'd been hearing it for a month, but I finally understood it myself. It wasn't any harmony or melody, or even rhythm, I was floating on out there. In a way it wasn't even music. I was talking, man. It was a voice, telling a long, forbidden story, an old story. I was a preacher man, in a way. All the rules were gone, you know. The bar lines, the keys, the little black notes, even the swing itself, all gone. It was just an old, endless story, and all it had to be was true. And it was coming through me, through that horn, through that little, rotting finger encased in glass and riding in my hip pocket. It was all of that. But it wasn't mine. It was the Story, and it was bigger than me.

I lost all track of time up there, but I guess now I must have played close to a couple hours. After a while, something happened that I never did before, you know. I started circular breathing. The air just seemed to float through me and into the horn in one long continuous breath, until I couldn't tell where my lungs ended and the reed began, until I couldn't tell where I was, other than bound to that horn. I was the instrument that the air played on with that horn. That's all it was, in the end. It was the air itself talking. I was just gone with all those old rules about keys and phrasing and tone for a while.

I didn't enchant that crowd the way I did those a people on the street, though. The musicians, man, they know about the tricks. Cats like that are too far into the how to get lost in some kind of wow. But I still had them. They were still in my hip pocket, man. Next to the Hands of the Bird.

I know I had them, not because I could see them. My eyes were closed. And I was gone anyway, man, lost in the night air. Even when I opened my eyes, I don't remember seeing a thing. But Ching told me, when I collapsed on the stage, for a long moment everyone sat still, not quite sensing that the music had really stopped yet. Then they didn't know what to do. She said they weren't sure if, after what I'd done up there, if I was still alive.

All I know is this: I came to and I was breathing, but only with a lot of work. Ching was hovering over me, and I could see Max behind her and then a lot of other faces. Michael Browning cleared the stage; his voice was the first thing I heard. "Give him room to breath," he was saying. "Back up, please. He just needs some air."

Ching was cradling her fist in one hand. "It's all right, Benny," she was whispering. "Just relax and breathe, easy." It was the wallop she gave me on the chest that brought me around and started me breathing again, but I didn't know that then.

"Is the kid okay?" Max was saying over and over, and looking around for Browning. "Michael, you didn't tell me your kid threw fits."

Ching got me up on my feet and Michael cleared a way to the stairs. He brought the case, and that was when I noticed the smell first, I think. I was afraid maybe I'd shit all over myself when I blacked out. But the way I reeked, the path upstairs cleared easily ahead of us. "Easy, easy, Benny," Ching kept whispering in my ear. I was leaning on her enough she was nearly carrying me, but I was really too heavy for her. Michael stepped up and bore some of my weight.

At the foot of the stairs, Rudy popped out of nowhere. He jabbed his fist out at me with the thumb up. "Killer, Benny," he said, nodding his glare at me. "Killer. Tomorrow night we go for it for real."

Michael was grinning, and he wrapped his free arm around my shoulder. "The streets are gonna be yelling about the Dove tonight, Benny. We're on our way. And you're gonna be just all right."

"Let's get him upstairs, Michael," Ching said. "Get him a cab."

The applause started about then. It might have been Rudy who started it first, but as Ching and Michael helped me up the narrow stairs, and the crowd realized I wasn't dead, their applause grew and grew.

"What is that smell?" Michael said, as we stepped out onto the street. Then I knew the stench. I heard the whistles and hoots behind us down in the basement club. The applause started then on the street, in that crowd too. I touched my pocket. "Nothing, Michael," Ching barked, as if she was embarrassed. "Get us a cab." But she knew what it was, I think, as I felt the broken vial in my pocket wrapped in Lucky's dirty handkerchief. I must have broken it open somehow when I fell, and let the Relic loose. It was the smell of old, rotten flesh. It was the sweet smell of death.

"How long did I play?"

We were alone now, in her round bed. Ching was holding me. Her long legs were wrapped around mine, and she held me tight with them. "I don't know," she said. "But Rudy had the tape running. He can tell us. Tomorrow."

"Did he get it all?" I said. "Even when I blacked out?"

The room was dark, but it seemed lit by her deep red sheets, and by the cobalt blue in her hair. And by the finger that was stuffed in an old perfume bottle and sitting on her night table in front of an oval mirror.

"I suppose," she said.

After we'd gotten rid of Michael Browning, Ching had undressed me. My leg was cut by the broken vial, and I'd bled a little, though we hadn't noticed it through those deep red pants. She threw the reeking stage clothes out her bay windows into the street. But only after she'd carefully removed the remains of the vial. She'd scattered perfume around the floor to kill the sweet stench, and then poured the rest of it down the sink in the bathroom. Then we stuffed the little relic into that clear, cut glass bottle that sat now, glowing in my mind like a candle in the night, sitting by the mirror. I seemed to gain some strength back once the finger was safe again, enclosed in that perfumed glass.

Then Ching undressed and filled the tub and we bathed together, washing the reek and its memory away. I was strong enough, afterwards, to carry her to the bed. We lay awake there, talking now and then, with her holding me tightly, for a long, long while in the night.

"You were right," she said.

"About what?"

"About the . . . what that . . . About what that thing can do," she said. The fear in her was new to me. She'd been hurt before, I'd seen that in her eyes when we made love. But I think to this very day that was the only time Ellen Ching had ever been afraid.

"What do you mean?" I said. We were both looking at the bottle that held the finger.

"You said the other night you thought it was why you couldn't breathe." Ching rested her hand on my shoulder. I saw the bruise at the base of her palm. It was the hand she'd beat my chest with, to keep me alive. "You said you thought it would kill you. If you let it."

I laughed, but I also pulled the red sheet around her naked shoulder. "I think it will," I said, after a while.

"Benny," she said to me and her voice dropped into a tiny, breathless whisper. "Benny, it was me. It wasn't your fall." Then she looked away from me at the bruise on her palm. "I broke the vial open, Benny. It was me, it wasn't any accident. You didn't fall on it." She bit her lip and she looked so beautiful gazing away from me. "I was afraid, Benny. You weren't coming around. You stopped breathing, and you even stopped trying to breathe. And I was pounding your chest and you were going and going. Then I remembered what you told me about that vial. About what you believed." Then she sucked in a long, long breath as if she was preparing to play a passage without end on an invisible horn. "I was afraid. So I broke it. I broke it open. With my hand."

"And I started . . . " I said, but Ching stopped me. She put a finger on my lips and wouldn't let me finish that thought.

Ching slipped over on top of me then, and she pinned me down on the bed. I could feel, as she moved, her fear ebb away. That bright smile rose to her lips, and its light stole me away from that perfumed vial by the mirror. She took me inside her and began to make love to me slowly, and she told me, "Wouldn't it be better, baby, to be stoned to death in the streets, than to just let the mills of this world grind you up in slow motion?" I didn't know what she was talking about. She moved in and around me, and sometimes held my arms pinned to the bed. Sometimes she stroked my chest with her bruised hand. "Benny, you can make the world hot for a while, or you can let it turn your minutes into penitentiaries, baby." Her voice became a sort of hoarse chant, a background as the world moved around me, a quiet, still song I held to while the big music in the sky rattled around like a machine, clanking its chains, gearing up to work. "Not everybody gets your choice, Benny. You're different than the rest of us. You're special, somehow. Baby, you can mint pure gold out of the rare, thin air you breathe, or you can spend your time scraping up copper pennies out of some foul, abstract shit in the streets. It's such a little price to pay, Benny," she said, moving over me in ways I couldn't see, didn't understand. "A little extra time, for a chance to reach the peaks up there, baby." She was laughing then, as she rocked gently over me. She kept talking and laughing, and she drove me crazy, as slowly as she could.

Finally I rolled her over and made love to her, and to that old relic and to Lucky who gave it to me, and to the big Music itself, clanking away above us. And when I was done, I fell over on my side and she was still laughing and talking to me, going on and on, saying things I didn't understand. Then Ching took our sweat in her hands and stroked me until we made love again. She bit my shoulder and drew blood in the end, and then finally she was quiet. She smiled and slept, her bruised hand cupped, cradling her cheek, sound asleep.

It was first light when I rose. I put on the chalk striped suit, quietly, in bathroom. When I was dressed I went to Ching's drawer in the kitchen. I found that bank bag, and I stole a fistful of bills from her. Big bills, too. I picked up my horn and the pork pie hat, and then I slunk back out into the bedroom. Without a second thought, I pocketed the perfume bottle by the mirror.

Ellen Ching was still asleep. The sheet had fallen down to her waist when I slipped out of bed. She lay there, naked and beautiful, breathing deeply in her dreams. She was biting her bottom lip. Her hand lay on the pillow where my head had been. I wanted to lean down and cover her to keep her warm, and I wanted to kiss her soft, black hair. But I didn't dare to wake her.

On the street I found a cabby nodding off from a long night shift, and he took me to La Guardia.

Four

It's a long story, how I got to Kansas City from there. Finding a seat on a morning flight and then walking around downtown all afternoon, trying to figure out who could tell me what I needed to know. Finally wandering on foot over to 18th and Vine. About dusk I found the big pink building that still houses the Musicians' Union, and there a woman told me how to find it.

It was raining in Missouri, and it was a cold dark night by the time I got to the cemetery. A cab dropped me off at the corner alone. I wandered in amongst the old stones, and realized my problem suddenly. Which one? There must have been an acre or two of old stones at the back of the cemetery. I'd be here for days trying to find it. And in the wet and the dark, it was hard to read the names.

I started off to one side along a wire fence and I worked in rows, leaning down to see each stone, reading out the last name. Sometimes I had to touch the old marble or granite, to read the name like it was Braille. I just felt for the first letter of the last name, and went on from there if I needed to.

A couple hours went by like that, in the rain and the dark. The sax in its case was growing heavy, and I was tired. The rain was starting to soak through the suit to my shirt. When the wind blew, it cut through me like it never did when I played under the old Pacific rains. I wasted a lot of time trying to read a couple of old markers. They were worn by the weather until the names and dates were faint.   But like a fool, I tried to read them anyway.

Then I heard Lucky's voice. "Little B.C.," he said. I stood up straight and looked around. There was nothing but rain and wind and wet gravestones. "Lucky?" I said. A hard chill ran through me, but there was still no Lucky around.

"You sure, Little B.C.?" his voice came again from right behind me.   "Remember now, boy, I asked you if you wanted it."

"Where are you?" I said, turning around. My shirt was drenched through now, but it might have been with sweat, because I was burning up suddenly.

"You could give it away, Benny, the way I did " his voice said.

"Where is it?"

The moment I said that, everything changed. A big gust of wind blew the rain back, and I saw him--or someone -over in the distance in front of me. Just a small, shadowy figure, really. But he waved to me. "Over here," Lucky said.

I slung the tenor case up on my shoulder again, and then broke into a run across the graveyard. The air seemed to grow still. "Lucky," I said, as I came near to him.

He was in the same pin striped suit, and his little gray mustache was trimmed more neatly than before, if that was possible. But he wasn't smiling to see me. He looked out at me sadly, from under his dark brow.

"I'm sorry," I said to him.

He laughed, and then shrugged his shoulders. "It will go on, Little B. C.," he said. "You can't kill it. You can help it along. But you can't kill it, Benny."

The memories came roaring back at me then, so I could feel them, you know. At that moment, I couldn't remember the music or how I played. But I could feel the weight of Lucky's old alto pulling me down again. Dragging me to the floor, like it did that night in the warehouse. I could feel my lips bleeding from the horn again, and my shoulder and chest ached again. I could feel myself next to Ching, gasping to breathe. I could feel the blackness above the Vanguard, and for the only time, I could feel the heel of her palm trying to beat my dead chest back to life.

"You can't kill it, Little B.C.," Lucky said. "It will go on. With you or without you, son. It will go on."

I heard the rats scuffling around again, scurrying to get away. I looked up at him, but he wasn't there. I was just standing next to a tall marker. A black stone angel rose out of it, and for a moment I expected her to speak to me. Her wings were curled up over her shoulders like she was ready to burst into flight. But she didn't. She was just an old gray stone, blackened with time and with rain.

The scuffling came at my feet again. Something bolted away from me into the cemetery, and then I saw the flat marker. I was standing on him, on a bare patch of mud where hundreds and hundreds of feet had worn the grass away, where the devotees of the Bird stood, over and over again. Just a flat, simple slab of stone, and it read easily, even in the dark. Charles Christopher Parker. 1920-1955.

I moved off to the side, under the black angel next to Bird's grave, and I tore up the grass. Then, bare handed, I dug a hole about a foot deep. When I figured it was deep enough, I opened up Ching's bottle and poured that crazy relic down into the ground. I didn't say any mumbo-jumbo words, no farewells. I didn't even think about much. I just heaped the sandy earth back in the hole and tamped it down with my foot. I dug out a piece of sod from behind the black angel, and fit it gently over my little part in his grave.

Then I took my horn out and put it together. It started to sleet then, but I still felt warm. I played for him, and for me too, I suppose. I played "I Concentrate On You." Chorus after chorus. And I never moved from the melody once. I just played the old, written notes straight. It wasn't that I didn't want to take off and fly. But it was as much as I could do. It was all I could do. "I Concentrate on You."

Until the police came. They figured I was drunk, disturbing the peace, out there wet and covered with mud playing away on a sax, the same old tune over and over, in an old cemetery at night. The sleet was piling up on my shoulders and on the bell of the horn. Maybe they were worried about me, too, you know. But I paid them with some of bills out of Ching's roll. So they dropped me off at the Westin downtown, because I told them I had a room there. Then I slept in an empty dumpster in the alley between the hotels down there, listening to the gentle rattle of the sleet over me, breathing easy.

I thumbed my way back West as winter swept over the High Plains and the Rockies. I was trying to save as much of Ching's roll as I could. It was my stake, you know? Time to start over, man. Just me and my lonesome, no magic fingers no more.

But I should have just spent the cash on a plane ticket. See, I got back to my one room in the Central District just in time to pay the late rent, and not get thrown out. Then I fell sick in bed for weeks, wound up in Harborview with pneumonia, my lungs filled with shit, until I lost the place and all that cash besides. I was down to my Lucky look-alike suit and my horn. But I refused to pawn that horn, man. It was my blood, you know? It had taken me all this way, through all of this. So I was broke and down to my sax, and that's when the hospital decided I was well enough. They could boot me back out in the street, to get sick all over again.

So like I say, for the rest of the winter I played in the streets. I lived in a two bucks a night mission, down in Pioneer Square, and I played outside the 'Sonics and the T-birds and the Huskies, and I got by. I saved my money so one day I could get a room somewhere of my own. But it seemed like I was just racing with the rents, you know. And losing.

One night I thought I saw Lucky, when I was playing outside the Arena. I followed him in his dark suit down the street, and I even broke into a run after him, toting my horn out in front of me awkwardly, when it seemed he'd slip away. In the end all I did was scare the wind out of an old Filipino man on his way to the opera. He was panting, trying to catch his breath, the whites of his eyes bright under the streetlights, and holding out his billfold when I caught up with him. I walked back to the awning in front of the Arena. Somebody had stolen the cash in my case, you know. The whole night of playing, gone like that. It was the pin stripe suit, you know. That's what fooled me.

Not long after that, I walked down from the mission toward the Kingdome one afternoon. It was quiet. Like always, I had the horn with me, you know. I wandered back through the warehouses and alleys until I found Lucky's place. I wasn't sure at first. The building looked different during the day, you know. Hand trucks and forklifts moving around, the warehouse was full of people hauling Japanese car parts from here to there. But I saw the walkway up above.

I found my way up into Lucky's room, and there was the same rat dust in the corners, and the same bald light bulb hanging from a wire. But there wasn't any old Selmer alto there. There was no music, just a desk and a guy chewing on an unlit cigar under the "no smoking" sign. "We ain't hiring, bud," he said. "Come back next week."

It's enough for me to be playing, though. Still, somehow, these days it isn't the same as it used to be. And it isn't the Vanguard and all the attention or anything, you know? It's just that, man, I heard once what a horn in my hands could play. I felt that talk rolling through me, and I was gone for a while, and the music was all that was out there. And, well, it's not the same anymore, you know? It just seems like it's all a lot of tunes these days, when I play. Good tunes, I know, but they're just tunes. For a time, it was the big story I was playing. You can't go back to where you were, man, not after that.

One afternoon I was thinking about these things while I was playing some song. I don't even remember what it was, you know. But I just quit playing then. Maybe for the day, and maybe for more than that. I should've kept at it that afternoon, because the tourists are back and my case was filling up with coins. But I just needed a rest, suddenly. There wasn't anything left for me to say. I thought, hey, it's spring, man. I'm going to hitch back out there to K.C. I'm going to go visit the grave, man, and then I'm going to get that magic spark back. Easy as that.

But then this guy in one of those gray suits came walking up. This suit, he'd been standing there drinking coffee and listening to me limp through some tune. Maybe it was because I had my suit on, and my pork pie hat. Maybe it was because he heard me play. But right when I quit, he comes walking up and takes out his card. Standing right in front of me, without saying a word, he writes something on the back and tosses it in my case with all the tips for the day. Then he winked at me and strolled away.

I picked up the card and read it. It made me think about how the hospital and my pneumonia and all, how it took everything away from me, because I didn't have any insurance or anything. That gray suit was named Richard Monroe. On the back of the card he wrote a date, and then he wrote that his company was needing agents. Turns out they needed some salespeople on the Peninsula, you know? It's a growing place out there, and people out there need insurance.

At the time, it seemed like maybe a good way to raise the bucks for my trip to K.C., you know. Coming when it did, there, just when I'd run out of music. So I got some money out of my stash and I took my suit to the cleaners. Then when I was looking sharp, I went downtown to Mr. Monroe's office and took this test last Thursday. The results are supposed to take a week. You see, anytime now I could be hearing from them. Anytime.

I used my middle name down there at the company, just on the outside chance anybody might have heard of me as player, you know? As far as Mr. Monroe is concerned, I'm Mr. B. David Crisp. Prospect.

That record came out this spring too. A two record set, man. "One Night Stand," Michael called it. In the liner notes he explained why it drops off so suddenly at the end. Rudy even put a disclaimer on it, apologizing for the sound, and blaming the trial conditions at the club. "Because of the sound difficulties and the live situation, this recording is for the specialist and the collector, and not for the general listener." That's what he wrote on the back.

They released it on a little label called Dovetone. In fact, it was Dovetone 001. What that means, you know, is Michael couldn't find any of the majors to take it. But I guess he still thought it was important enough it should be issued. For history, or something. I bought the only copy I ever saw in town. But I still haven't heard it. I set it on my shelf at the mission, sort of like a bowling trophy. But I haven't told anybody it's me on there.

You know, on the inside of the album it said that Benny Crisp, who was called the Dove in jazz circles, had mysteriously dropped out of sight. He was known to suffer from serious epileptic fits, possibly from problems with past drug abuse. He hadn't been seen since the night the recording was made, which left his friends and admirers concerned about his condition, and about the possibility of foul play. "If anyone knows anything about the whereabouts of the Dove," Michael's line notes ended, "please contact Dovetone Records."

Yesterday, just for old time's sake I guess, or maybe because I was trying to figure this all out, I took my sax and went back up to the banking district. I was even wearing my suit, you know, and feeling pretty lucky, too. But when I got up there on the Ave, I didn't really want to play. I knew without trying how I would sound, you know. See, I'd buried all my magic back in the ground in K.C. So I just stood there for a while, watching all those busy people scurry by, to all those places they had to be, and I reminisced about the way I'd stopped them all, right in their footsteps, right in the middle of the street. It was a good thing, you know, what I did. These people they need to stop, man, and wrap their heads around something that doesn't have to do with money. They need a vacation from the real bucks, man. And that was me, you know. Back then. But now, on a good day, I'm spare change.

It was right there, at that moment when I was thinking about all those suits and about Mr. Monroe and the Company, I saw her again. I swear it was her, man. I know it was her. She was strutting down the sidewalk across the street, and all in black leather again, you know. And those heads were snapping to look at her, as she strolled on by.

I slung the sax case over my shoulder, crossed in the middle of the street, and followed her for a few blocks. I guess I wasn't really sure what to do, you know. Because I wasn't the Benny Crisp she knew before, man. I wasn't the Dove, anymore. But I still couldn't help myself.

I caught up with her in front of the same hotel we'd slept in, man. She was turning to go inside those big glass doors, and she'd be gone in a minute, you know? It was like forever, right then and there. I couldn't just let her disappear suddenly gone. "Ellen," I said. I don't know why, because I'd never called her that before.

Ching turned, her hand resting on the thick brass handle to the door, and she looked right at me. The blue streak in her hair was gone. It seemed wrong to not have it there. I wanted to touch her hair and make that beautiful cobalt blue come back. And her look, it was blank, man. "Yes?" was all she said. There was no bright smile to wrinkle the corners of her yes. There was nothing. And I realized all at once how far I'd lost her.

She reached in her bag and pulled out a handful of change and tossed it to me. Spare change, man, like I was a bum or something. I let it clatter on the sidewalk at my feet. But Ching never saw that. By the time the coins hit the concrete, she'd already disappeared through those big whirling doors.

I suppose that's when I made my biggest mistake of all. The biggest screw up of my many, many mistakes. But it's a hard thing to let go, in the end, you know? I'm learning that. Slowly.

I stood a moment, one hand wrapped around the strap of my tenor bag, the other just stuck in the empty pocket of my suit jacket. Then I made the stupid move. I followed her into the lobby. Ching was already long gone, nowhere to be seen, man. So I got into an elevator and rode it up as far as it would go. But it just stopped at the twelfth floor. I needed that key of hers--the one that came from nowhere in all her black leather--to get to the top, to reach those skylights where she lived. But I had no way up there. Not anymore.

Still, I wouldn't give up. I hadn't learned yet.

I rode back down and walked over to the desk in the lobby and asked for her. "Could you call Ms. Ellen Ching and tell her the Dove is here to see her?" I said to the guy at the counter. He smiled with just his lips. "The Dove?" he muttered, nodding his head, with one hand flipping through the registry and the other resting on this pure white phone. He was wearing a suit almost as nice as mine, if a little cleaner.

His smile disappeared for an instant. Then it was back. "There's no one by that name registered here, sir," he said, looking up from a screen behind the counter.

"But I just saw her come in," I said.

He raised his eyebrows and the flat little smile came back to just his lips. Then he repeated what he just said.

"Listen," I let my grip on the sax bag's strap tighten, and tried to say calm. "I know she's like, you know, some sort of VIP, or something. It's probably confidential, right? That she's here? But if you just call up and give her that message, that the Dove is here to see her, man, everything will be cool. Trust me, guy, would you?"

He just repeated himself. The brows dropped and the smile seemed like I'd imagined it.

"Buddy," I said, "I know she's up there in that big room with the skylights. The one on the roof, man. She knows who I am. Call her up, okay?" I found my hand had loosed itself from the strap and I was pointing at him with my finger.

Then Ms. Robinson showed up. Her name was on the little black and gold tag she wore that said she was head of hotel security. She's a tall blonde lady, about as square as a fullback, with a grin that was fixed on the side of her face and only seemed to shift between sneer and snicker. "We have a problem, Jim?" she said to the counter. Then after a little explanation, she held my elbow and escorted me gently outside to the street.

I waited for her to leave, then walked around the block to another door. I guess with every step I took on that sidewalk, I convinced myself I needed to see Ching more and more and more. She became some kind of last chance for me, or something, you know?

So I snuck back in by another door, and found a service elevator near a backstairs to the basement. Even on that, I could only get to the twelfth floor. So I climbed out up there and found a stairwell at the end of a hall.

A fire door inside it was locked from my side and it said something in red and black about employees only. But it had a window in it, you know, about a foot square, with the kind of glass that's swallowed some wire mesh. I took the butt end of my sax case and shoved it right through the window. All my first shot did was crack that pane in two places, then it took another couple of rams to break the glass and wire out. It tore up the leather on my gig bag some, but the horn was all right inside, I think. It was one pretty tough flight case I had. I set the horn and the case down in the corner then, if I remember right.

I was on my tiptoes, with my arm stuck through the broken window and trying to reach the door latch and push it down inside, when Ms. Robinson showed up. She wore the same sneer that switched its snicker off and on. And she had two plainclothes guards with her this time, when she led me away by the elbow again. We all rode straight back down that same service elevator I'd found to a little room in the basement. I don't remember anybody carrying my saxophone though. We left it up there, I think. But I don't know, man, because I wasn't really myself right then, you know?

On the way Ms. Robinson recited my rights at me; she knew them by heart, of course. Then I sat at a desk beside her while she filled out a lot of paperwork. The other two guards were gone somewhere, they just left us alone. I tried to tell her who Ching was, and how I knew her, and all that. She nodded and sneered a little softer, and didn't believe me.

It took about forty-five minutes for the police to show. They hauled me away and held me for a couple hours. I know the police were uptown at the office in their files fingering through my old record, figuring I was just another old time junkie wigging out on them. They were looking for a way to lock me up for a long while.

But then I got a surprise. It happened quickly too. The hotel, suddenly, decided not to press charges against me. After all of this mug shot and fingerprint circus, the cops just came downstairs and let me go. I was clean, and suddenly I was free. Freer than I thought I'd be for a long, long while.

I know Ching was behind it all. She's the one who set me free. She's the one who paid to fix that broken glass. It's one of the ways I know that it was really her I saw on the street. She sprung me loose, man. I know she did.

I rode a bus back uptown to the hotel, and Robinson was there in the lobby when I walked in.

"Haven't you been lucky enough for one day?" she said, holding my elbow again.

I shook my head. "Man, I'm just here to get my horn back."

She frowned and her little sneer disappeared for the first time since we'd met. "You had something with you?" she said.

"A couple of grand worth of saxophone," I said.

She looked worried, and I sort of liked her for the first time. After all, she was just doing her job, right? Robinson made some calls from the reservation desk, while I stood around. Then she shrugged at me, and we rode the service elevator back up to my twelfth floor stairwell. A couple of workers were bolting heavy glass back in the door, the glass Ching must have paid for, but there wasn't any saxophone anywhere, man. Gone.

"We've got no record of it, Mr. Crisp,"
Robinson shrugged again. "It's not anywhere in the
paperwork."

Back in the lobby, she told me to check with
her tomorrow. "I'll look into it," she said, then the
little sneer crept back onto her face. "But you know
how easy it is to hock a saxophone, I'm sure," she
said. "You carry any insurance on it?"

Ellen Ching, or that woman who looked just
like her, stepped out of an elevator into the lobby
then. She walked smoothly across the dark rugs on
the floor and disappeared through one of the heavy
glass doors. I heard her heels touch the tiles in the
entryway from clear across the room, and those
doors made a soft whoosh as the warm air rushed
out behind her. She turned her head one way on the
street, and then the other, so saw her profile twice.
The second time I saw it, the pretty lines around her
eyes wrinkled up and her white, shining smile
appeared, man, like a spotlight on a dark, basement
stage. Then she turned her head back, she stepped
off the curb and went away.

"Call me tomorrow about it," Ms. Robinson
was saying.

But like I say, that was all yesterday and I've
had time to think it all over now. The only phone in
the mission here is downstairs in the lobby, and I
should go down there right now and call, instead of
sitting here.

But I've learned a lot in these last few hours
sitting by myself on this cot. I've learned a lot
about how you take your chances, about your

obsessions, man, and whether you follow them or you run away from them. About breathing the thin air of your own sweet risks, and about the price you got to pay to be up there where mistakes are bright and the lights are thin. About what it costs to touch that cobalt blue that runs like a vein of gold through our time. Everything you do, babe, it's got to be earned, you know? Even when the spark is tossed your way, man, when the touch is in your fingers, and your hands speak in tongues. Even when somebody who isn't even thinking about being fair, has handed you the gift. Even when you're touched by the saints. You still got to earn your way. And there's a letter came in the mission's mail for me today. The one I been waiting for, from Mr. Monroe and the Company. Here's what I'm going to do. I'm gonna open it up, and then maybe I'll go downstairs.

The Lady in the Cameo

She closed her eyes and held them closed, but she couldn't sleep. Her head lay against the wall of the coach, and she could feel the train pulling sleeplessly out of the station. It rattled and bumped and razed her head against the metal wall. She told herself it was the jostling of the train that kept her awake. But she knew better.

She knew better about a lot of things, and leaning there with her eyes closed she couldn't fool herself about any of them. She couldn't sleep, it was the middle of a black rainy night late in the winter and she was riding a train bound for someplace she didn't want to be, for some piece of prairie grass Robert had bought in Texas, and now she was pregnant for the third time, and she was only twenty-four. There was still an ache around her eyes that meant she was carrying a fever. It left her tired at the same time it wouldn't let her sleep. And not love nor loyalty nor luck was going to stop that train and let her rest.

But the boys were both asleep, finally, and that was a blessing.

Lucy got up and went to the bathroom again, and the specks of blood were still there. Looking at herself in the cracked mirror, she felt weak and her breath was hot against her nostrils. She looked at her eyes and saw all the redness there too.

"I wish I could just get some sleep," she whispered aloud, to no one in particular.

Walking down the aisle she reminded herself that there were no cramps, just that her stomach was upset. There would have to be cramps. That's what she'd heard when Agnes Kehoe lost her baby.

Agnes was the lucky one now. It was their first baby that the Kehoes lost, and then Kevin was born early too. They had such trouble to have a son. When Kevin was born it seemed he almost dragged out Agnes's intestines with him. The midwife had to take Agnes's insides and stuff her back together. But Agnes Kehoe was lucky enough to be barren after that.

Lucy sat down in the empty seats across the aisle from where the boys slept, because she didn't want to sit next to them now. In order not to see them, she watched what she could out the window.

The train pushed along through a break in the trees then. The coach tilted downhill. They were running along the river suddenly, and she could see the water almost level with the tracks. A barge floated out on the Mississippi; she saw the pale yellow of its lanterns through the mist and rain. Lucy couldn't see the tug though, whether it was pushing upstream or sliding down. But then the train pulled up an incline and they ran back in against the dark of the trees. For a long while the train kept pulling uphill, so she knew they were headed away from the river.

Outside there was nothing but dark trees in the rain. Against the dark, the dim light of the electric lamps in the coach reflected yellow in the window, and she saw her face in the glass. The reflection wasn't clear. All the exact detail was gone, slipping into the shadows inside and the blurred dark of the moving countryside, so what was left was an impression of her face, a yellow image that highlighted her features. She saw how pretty she was when all the details were erased, as if she'd left her sharp edges in the clear glass of the restroom. Her black hair, as curly and wild as ever, had come loose and framed her face in a black that was darker than the dark outside. The slate gray of this hobgoblin mirror gave her pale skin a swarthy color she liked.

Men had always admired her skin. Once, when she was young, the summer would give her a rosy color that was warm and pretty, a perpetual blush in a world of eyes. But ever since Vince was born, that shade never came back.. She kept a cold winter pale all year around. So now Lucy admired her dusky looks in the window; her eyes were hidden in the dark of her skin. It was not the color of any farm girl.

There was an impurity in the glass, a wave that distorted her face. If she turned her head, her face stretched sideways. Another twist and she was a long warped smear of blue. Lucy turned her head this way and that, playing with her reflection and rebuilding her face.

She tried a longer nose and a shorter chin; she sat higher in her seat so she could give herself fat high cheeks like a big boned Swedish woman; with a thrust of her head she could make her eyes disappear. She was stretching her eyebrows higher in the glass, when suddenly her eyes grew terribly small and her brow folded into a brutish lump, and Lucy saw something she didn't want to see. She sat back in the seat and closed her eyes again.

Her own refection in the window had reminded her of that poor little boy Emily Counter had. Emily had never married, so she was called an old maid back home. But then one day, when she was forty or so, she left Maquoketa. She'd had enough of all the talking and moved to Chicago, people said. Just two years later Emily came home to her father's big empty house at the end of Tyler Street and had a baby.

Miss Counter had a boy, born with a head larger than his body, and a face as small as his hands. She used to bring him to church on Sunday, with a lady's bonnet covering his head, and everyone tried to ignore it all when she had to leave Mass early every week, because whenever the choir started to sing the prayers in Latin, the boy started moaning so loud you couldn't concentrate on the altar anymore. And then he'd start spitting on the people in the pews around them. That little child actually lived to be one or two years old, and never even learned to stand up.

Sometime after the burial, Emily Counter left her father's house. No one knew exactly when for sure.   People thought maybe she'd gone back to Chicago.   It was Herb Finney who was out coon hunting that fall and found her, months later, living in a cave on the Muskwego River, half starved to death and talking to herself about the restaurants on Lake Shore Drive.

A curse and a punishment, some people said. Let it be a lesson to these young women. But Lucy had wondered from the start if a child could be born for no reason other than to be a punishment on someone else, and a lesson for the rest of us. Seemed like maybe there were other lessons in what happened, lessons they were missing.   But Lucy couldn't say what they were.   She didn't know what they were.

With a sharp rattle the train rose again and they went over a bridge. They crossed another river, smaller and vague in the misty rain.   It was gone before Lucy made much note of it.   She avoided looking out the window now, and wished she could sleep.

About half a dozen seats away, Corallis Bean was reading something she held in her lap.   Lucy knew it had to be her Bible, of course. This woman did nothing but stare at that book.

Lucy still had the pictures in her pocket, the postcard photos of Texas that old woman had handed her without a word.   Moments ago it all seemed like too much of a chore: to return them to her. The less she saw of that fierce old woman, the better. It was the two boys who had taken a liking to pestering her about Texas.

But now Lucy stood up and pulled out the crumpled envelope that held the cards, and she walked up the aisle, lazily letting the fingers of her left hand touch and rest on they back of each seat along the way. Lucy was right. Mrs. Bean was reading the same worn Bible, and the woman did not look up when Lucy's fingers rested on the edge of the seat near her shoulder. In fact, she covered the page she was reading with her hand.

Lucy said, "I enjoyed your pictures, Mrs. Bean." The old woman slowly raised her head and stared blankly at her. Lucy held the worn envelope out to her, but Corallis Bean made no move to take it.

"They're really very nice, and they did give me an idea of where were going." Corallis Bean stared at her without any sign she understood, until Lucy lowered her arm with the letter still in her hand. "Would you mind if I sat down?" Lucy asked.

Slowly the old woman looked over at the seat across from her, her breath wheezed in her nose, and then a smile glowed up into her eyes and creased her cheeks with oddly familiar lines. She snapped the Bible shut with a crack.

"Please do," she said, too brightly.

But Lucy sat down facing her anyway and settled her green dress on the seat around her. When she looked up, the smile on Corallis Bean's face had disappeared, the comfortable wrinkles were entirely gone, and in their place were the lines of an old woman.

"It sounds like your son is doing well in Texas," Lucy said, immediately regretting it. She had betrayed her reading of the letter she found in the envelope with the pictures. It was from Mrs. Bean's son, a minister in Houston, coaxing and cajoling her to come and live in Texas. It was the only way, her son pleaded. Otherwise, if she stayed in Milwaukee, Corallis Bean would have to go live in a home, it said. "That home" were the words he used.

"Yes," the old woman said, "he's very happy there. And he thinks that I'll like it." She was quiet for a long moment, and Lucy heard the woman's foot tap briskly once against the floor of the car.

"We'll see," she said.

"Well, these pictures sure make Texas look like a wonderful place," Lucy said.

The old woman nodded her head, but she seemed confused. She hummed two descending notes that came from no song. Then her eyebrows raised in a kindly way.

"You're pregnant?" Corallis Bean said, out of nowhere.

Lucy was surprised. She didn't think she showed yet. She hadn't even told Robert for fear he would give up his big plans, so her own husband hadn't noticed yet. "Yes," she said. "Yes, I am."

Corallis glanced at Lucy's dress lying against the gray of the seat. Her hand moved as if she wanted to touch it, but then it just touched her slate gray hair and rested back on her own black dress.

"I'm not very far along," Lucy smiled. "How did you notice? I'm not showing yet, am I?" she said.

The old woman shook her head no.

"It's still very early, you know, but I've had two already. Oh, of course, that's pretty obvious. You've met them. They've been bothering you all day," and she laughed at herself, at the way she could run at the mouth. But it felt good to talk.

"This time I'm a little worried though," she said. "Just today I had some trouble. How many children did you have? Just the one? If you don't mind me asking"

Corallis Bean didn't answer. Her brows just furled up and she looked frightened of something. Then she mumbled a word or two that Lucy couldn't catch.

"Excuse me. I shouldn't be so nosey," Lucy backed off. "It was rude of me. I just thought that . . ."

The old woman interrupted her very quietly. But what she said was garbled. Lucy leaned forward, trying to hear her, and reached over to touch the old woman's shoulder.

But when the hand came near, the old woman's anxious gaze stopped Lucy still. Then Corallis Bean hissed at her, "Don't you hear all the drummers whispering?"

Instinctively Lucy sat back in the seat. Long seconds passed, and quickly Lucy's confusion turned to fear, and then the fear to embarrassment, and she began to wonder how she could get back to her own seat without making some huge scene. She looked away from the woman, toward the floor, and momentarily tried to ignore her.

"He's down there," Corallis Bean said to her and her voice lowered into almost a growl. Then the old woman sighed loudly. "There's going to be bare places by the Nile, right up on the banks," she said loudly.

Corallis Bean shook her head in disgust. Then she stared directly into Lucy's eyes, holding them with the fervor of her glare, and nodded her head to emphasize every important word. "He's going to cut off the shoots with a pruning fork." The old woman paused, and her mouth moved to make unsaid words. Then she spoke again loudly, "And there will be fire around the well holes." In a final silence, her mouth set firmly into a frown.

Lucy laid the envelope of photographs beside the woman, and she pushed them softly until they slid down into the seat. Then she began to sidle her way toward the aisle, her dress wrinkling beneath her with every inch she moved on the bench seat. She kept thinking the whole while of how easy Robert's life was. He just rode along back there with the freight and the livestock and planned what he was going to plant on his big Texas farm, and never had to deal with squirming children or crazy old women. Or all the rest. But as she slipped near the end of the seat, Lucy was stopped by a sharp pain in her abdomen.

The old woman just sat there now and stared at her own knees, and ever so slightly nodded her head to some strange rhythm, different from the relentless rolling of the train. Corallis Bean still clasped the Bible tightly in her left hand. Lucy saw the black night outside through the coach window, silhouetting the old woman's profile like some sort of bleak cameo.

Then Lucy turned back. She leaned over and took the old woman's right hand in both of her own, still wondering what exactly she should say. The pain in her center had eased as quickly as it had come over her. The hand she held was meek and warm and alive, and despite the way Corallis Bean glared sternly into her own lap, the hand gently wrapped around hers.

"It will be all right," she said. The old woman made no sign she had heard. "Texas will be good," Lucy said, and squeezed her hand reassuringly.

When she let go, that frail hand slipped away from her, closed into a fist and sat rigidly in the lap of the woman's black dress. Then the train rattled over a break in the tracks, and the tiny, electric lights blinked, off and then on, and then off again.

Sirens

for John Carter

This is a story that ends with the sound of a clarinet. Or maybe I should say it begins there. At least life as anyone else would know it was born for me in the song of a clarinet.

Seems everybody wants to hear a guitar, or a saxophone, the honking brass, the screeching strings. But the clarinet, for Jan Bulkowski, is the sound of life itself. The sound of life returning.

I work at the Mail Box these days. I have for the past five years been the quiet guy behind the counter there, building boxes around other people's problems. They're coming in with some oblong mirror that needs to be shipped, or some tiny fragile electronic part, and I'm the guy who helps them pack it all safely away to be shipped to nieces and nephews, business partners on the road, or the enemy. Wherever they want. Whatever they want.

Of course, I sell them insurance on their special parcels, too. But a lot of times it isn't money they're sending. It's great-grandfather 's pocket watch with an antique, smoked glass face, or the moldering family portrait painted in the old country last century, or it's a handwritten manuscript like this one. These are the truly valuable things.

They buy insurance because, somehow, they think it means we'll pay more attention. Their investment of money will be transformed into our care and concern. They don't want insurance money. They want that watch to arrive safely at its destination in the grand nephew's pocket, with the smoked glass polished and unbroken. They want him to be able to find it and call back to them on time from the too far away place he lives now. They want that manuscript, those pieces of their own blood and viscera, to find its readers for all of time.

They don't know the UPS.

Last week, when it was slow one day at the Mail Box, I went in back to the storage room where the packages wait until the truck arrives, and I built a kit out of cardboard. Different size boxes will resonate, you know. I haven't figured out how to get a snare to work, but I could rig the boxes up like a row of tom-toms.

Some of the plywood from our crating material worked for sticks. I just split a length of it in half so it would fit in my hand better.

Then I propped myself up against a wall and used the corner of a desk for a stool, and I let loose. I was all alone in back, so nobody really knew. It felt good, even on that goofy, toy kit, to feel the roll of the drumsticks on my fingers again. I let loose with a couple of bursts, and kept the time with the toe of my foot against a big box. The response was pretty dull, but it felt so fine to be stretching out again. I could almost hear the horns soloing out in front of me, and in my mind Billie Holiday was waiting in the wings, but of course, I was facing the wall.

Even though the cardboard response was dull, at best, I must have made some noise. Bernie came running into the shipping room. She thought something terrible had happened. "Johnny!" She still thinks my name is John. "Johnny!" she said, "Are you okay?"

When she saw me with my little row of different sized boxes propped against the wall, she said, "What are you doing?" Bernie, more than anything, wants to work for United Parcel. She likes to think of herself as a manager at the Mail Box. And she takes supervising us all pretty damn seriously. She's a little, fat lady, but her heart is big and fat, you know? "You don't have enough to do, Johnny?" she asked. "You better put that stuff away and sweep up back here, or something."

She didn't say anything like, "I didn't know you played the drums?" Not anything like that. But she was right. I needed to get back to work.

Even if it did feel good, that row of cardboard heads splayed out in front of me, the bounce of those plywood sticks in my hands, the time beating in my right foot.

Even if it did feel good, I know, that way perdition lies. Perdition, I say. Perdition.

Now the concrete pavement is cold to my hand as I lean up against the curb. I don't feel the cold in the air, or anywhere down the whole length of my side where I'm lying on the pavement. Just the flat of my hand pressed against the cold concrete.   Shattered glass is still stuck on my clothing.   The back of my hand matches the black dust in the street.   It disappears into the dirt against the curb like some kind of chameleon made of filth. I am a lizard.   Dirty enough to be invisible.   When you are invisible, you can't be heard.   You can disappear into the general roar.

Then some cop leans down over me.   He's wearing a heavy blue coat buttoned up tight around his neck.   "Eri auy elroght, bydda?" he says.   I grin at him.   I know if you smile they think one of two things about you: they think you can   understand them or they think you're drunk enough that you're okay.   "Auy bittir git ap uat of thi strit, bydda, ur auy'll git hot," the cop says, out of all the loud jabbering around me.

I keep grinning and get up slowly on my knees.   Then he reaches out and puts his gloved hand firmly on my shoulder.   I feel his hold closing on me.   So I break loose and I run and run and run.

Car horns blow, a siren whines off in the distance, lost in the rows and rows of tall buildings. Some suits and ties stumble into me on the sidewalks, too.   They don't know which way to go, and they yell out when I touch them.   "Haii," the say. But the cop doesn't follow, though I hear him yelling out to me over the crowded streets for a while. What they don't know is this: I like it now.   All their horns and yelling and noise drowns out the roaring behind me.

Finally I stop in an alley and lean up against a dumpster there in the dark.   I sit so I can see out to the street and the daylight, in case anybody comes after me into the alley. It is snowing a little, and my palm still feels cold. But not the back of my hand. It is dark and warm as dust.

Then the whispers start up again.

I was just a kid. It was 1956, and I was seven years old. I didn't know she was Billie Holiday. Back then didn't know who Billie Holiday was. All I knew was my Uncle Leo got me backstage at Carnegie Hall. Leo was old, you know, so old he had more wrinkles than hair. He came across to America in the twenties, but when he left Poland on his great adventure, he was no youngster. No, he already had a wife, my Aunt Anastasia, and two daughters, Theresa and Katrina. Leo came across on a boat, landed in New York, and took any job and as many jobs as he could find.

Leo always liked to tell the story about sleeping in Central Park at night, and about stuffing old newspaper in his shoes to keep warm. But he made his way, Uncle Leo, though he never got rich. "Every cent I made," he used to say, "I used it to get you here."

But I wasn't around then. I wasn't even anybody's idea yet. Uncle Leo meant that by working two or three jobs at once, he could live at work, pretty much. So he saved on rent and only kept a room to wash up in on the Sundays he took off, and he sent the money back to Warsaw. By the time the hard days hit, Aunt Anastasia and the two girls were here, and then Uncle Leo's kid brother came across. His kid brother Max was my pop.

It's enough to make you wonder what with that story, how a kid like me, Jan Bulkowski, could wind up out on the street running wild. Could wind up just the same as my Uncle Leo, only he was fresh off the boat. 'What could make something like that happen?' you might be saying to yourself.

It isn't what you think.

By the time I was a scrapping around kid, Uncle Leo had his job at Carnegie. He got a real kick out of getting me inside. I got to come backstage with him and watch the stage door. And because of that I got to hear some great stuff. Isaac Stern and Yehudi Menuhin, and Lenny Bernstein a bunch of times. Uncle Leo would always put me up on the bench and get me to say, "Hello, Mr. Bernstein," and the Maestro, being a young guy himself, would always say to me, "Lenny, kid. Call me Lenny." Uncle Leo got a hot charge off of that, every time.

Most of it was classical stuff I heard, and that was great. But the time I remember most was that time when I was seven. It was a big tribute to Ms. Holiday, and they were reading from her book. She'd sing, and then some guy would read some, and then she'd sing some more.

When I look back on it, with what I know now, that was a pretty amazing group of cats gathered together that night. Coleman Hawkins was there playing that grand tenor of his filled with high dignity, looking like the royalty he was.

Eldridge played alongside him in the first set. In the second set, Buck Clayton and Kenny Burrell were on the bandstand. I went out and bought the record cut from the show, years later, though I don't know where it is now, don't know where it was left. At the time when I was a kid, like I say, I didn't know who any of these people were. I was just a little Polish kid from Brooklyn, age seven, scuffling around with his proud old Uncle.

But I do remember this. I heard the first tune from the stage, and I was drawn away from Uncle Leo and the back door. Uncle Leo was holding a finger to his lips, reminding me to be quiet, and I was just drawn away from him toward the wings of the stage, just like a little white moth pulled toward the flickering, golden flames.

Now, understand this: I'd heard Maria Callas. I'd heard Yehudi Menuhin. It was a kick. It was fun to go peek out at the spectacle, and at all the people in the crowd with their fancy tuxes and gowns. But I heard the first strains coming from Ms. Holiday and her band, and it was all I could do to keep from walking right out onto the stage.

Most of all, I heard the drums. With all those great musicians out there, and Billie Holiday herself singing, what I heard was the kit. It was nothing splashy, no solos or big old tom-tom beats. It was just solid, smooth riding swing that pulled the whole band along like the engine of an on-schedule train. Just a little riding on the cymbal, and some quiet, sweet fills from the brushes, and all that easy driving swing. It was Chico, man, I knew who he was later. I knew very well. It was Chico, man, and for me that was it.

Now I slip down and sit behind the dumpster, so no one can see me from the street. The alley is quiet in a way that the avenue out there never will be. The whispers now can roar at me as they will. But the dumpster is clean and new, a bright Kelly green. I rest my shoulder against it and watch the snowflakes land on the bright, shiny green. Some of them melt, and some of them stick to the seams and corners of it. I try to ignore their roaring. The flakes that melt darken and then turn to the bright green of the bin, and then they're gone. But the flakes that last, they stay as white and pure as when they fell from the sky. So the little pieces of falling sky gather together into feathery little piles collecting in the green corners and braces.

Some of them land on my hands, and these fade into gray slowly, and soak into my skin. I hold my hand out flat, to catch as many as will fall. If enough of them gather in the creases of my knuckles, I think they will learn to stay white and survive, just as they do on the shiny green dumpster.

My nails are long and they're darker than the back of my hand. All of them are broken, except the pinky. That one nail seems to keep growing and be safe. It is as long as the end of my finger now. Not like my thumbnail, which is split almost the length of the nail, from the tip of my thumb all the way back to the edge of my cuticle. Part of the thumbnail, one side of the split, is long and has curled around the tip of my thumb. I turn my hand and see how the nail has turned a yellow like old paper there at the curled tip. The other half of the nail is broken off so I can't see quite where it ends and where my thumb begins. Down the straight line of the split, a stripe of black crust has oozed out of me and dried. When I touch it with my first finger, the soft pain feels good. It feels like the pressure being eased out of a full bike tire.

If I hold my hand out very still, and stop picking at that split in my thumbnail, the snowflakes that happen to fall right on that stripe of ooze stick. They don't melt right away like they do when they happen to land on the rest of my hand.

It's a start. If I move my hand quickly enough, I can catch the snow there on the split in my nail, and the snow will last, will begin to pile up, and some day drift away.

It is a start.

During the intermission I was still standing there behind the curtain, and all the musicians were milling around backstage. I just kept looking out at the drum kit sitting alone on stage by the piano, and the bass lying on its side. The red and blue stage lights, even though they were low, caught on the chrome of the drum stands and the brass of the cymbals. The drums seemed to be built out of mother of pearl.

Then the lights went up and the musicians all sauntered out. The applause started smattering and then blossomed huge into catcalls and cheers and whistles. Even this guy who just read the words from the book created a swell in the clapping when he walked out, swaggering and grinning.

I don't know when she came up beside me, or how long she'd been standing there. I was too keyed in to every move that Chico Hamilton made out there to notice her. He picked up his sticks from somewhere they'd been magically stored on the kit. Then he wiggled the stool forward and then back a touch, while he tightened a few keys here and checked the angle of a cymbal there.

Her hands were about even with my shoulders. They were trembling. I think that I felt the air around her quaking, not that I saw her tremble. I felt it in an aura around her.

But I never stopped watching Chico as he now sat quietly and a little slumped behind the drum kit. I reached over and took her hand. It was just an instinct, you know. She was trembling so, it was just a seven year old kid holding her hand because she was scared. It wasn't any statement. I didn't know enough to tell her, "Don't be scared. You're great. You're Billie Holiday." Hell, at the time I didn't know who she was. It was just one kid beside another kid on some big strange playground. It was just a sense that none of us is ever alone. The sense you have as a kid, naturally, but it's too hard to hang onto, so easy to lose faith in: that we're all together. It's so easy to get lost.

I never looked up at her. My eyes were frozen on the way the hot lights played off the cymbals. She never looked down at me. Not even a glance, as far as I could tell. But her hand wrapped around mine, and squeezed it so tightly, it might have hurt if I hadn't been so wrapped up in the drums. Most of all, because she was squeezing my hand so hard, her hands stopped trembling.

At first, I was sort of startled, and I thought I should be afraid. But then Chico hit a soft splash on the cymbal and went into a roll with his brushes on the snare, and the reader guy announced her name. She let go of my hand, and walked out on stage like royalty. She was beautiful, but she seemed so old and frail. I could still feel the press of her hand around mine, could still feel her desperation. It made me want to run away, because I didn't understand how someone so beautiful and loved and stately could be so desperate and afraid. Life wasn't supposed to be like that, maybe for Uncle Leo and for me, but not for the beautiful, not for the loved. Not for the Lady. That was when she looked back at me, in the wings. It was just a glance. But it has taken me the rest of my life to learn what that glance meant, the depth of the gratitude in it.

She began to sing, and it was "Yesterdays" that she sang about. She never looked over at me again, but she stood and held the whole crowd like a lover. She began the tune as happy and light as could be, it was almost Dixieland in its fervor. But as the choruses came back again, she slowed it gradually down, until it ended almost as a lament, certainly as the blues. It was a mighty transformation. Then she sang "Please Don't Talk About Me When I'm Gone." Without a pause, she slipped right into it. Not even Chico Hamilton's swing could hold me then. Her despair and her gratitude and the fierce love all around her was more than I could take, at that age. I don't know that I could take it now. I ran back out past Uncle Leo, and scared him in the process. Then I stood in the alley by the stage door, trying to catch my breath.

When you're just a kid, you can't believe your life could be like that, you can't believe that all those dreams can turn to blasted hopes and lost desires and the fear of tomorrow. It just sits there, inside you, when you're pure like a child. But when you take it by the hand, and feel it gripping you, pulling at you for help, well, you're still too young to know what it is to have your breath stolen away. You run and you hide, because such beauty and the pain that accompanies it shouldn't hold you like that, like the lover's hand of fear itself, like the hand of Billie Holiday.

Inside it now there is some lettuce and a couple tomatoes going bad. And there are a lot of scraps of old hamburger patties. The dumpster is only about half full, so it is a long reach down inside to find the food. It is dark in there.

I hoist myself up until the rim of the dumpster is about at my waist and then I lean over slowly. This way, I am leaning down into it, but my legs and butt and all are still hanging out. I grab a couple big handfuls of food and then just sort of fall back out, landing on my feet, and then I sit down on the ground to examine the take.

The hamburger meat has some white fuzz growing on one side of it, so I throw it aside. The lettuce, though, I can peel off the brown and wilted leaves, and inside it is pretty good. There are some little white bugs running around down by the stalk, but if I just eat the center of the leaves, they can have the rest. The two tomatoes I grabbed are soft, and there is bad spot on one of them. So I bite into the one that seems all right, except for a little quarter inch slice by the stem. The tomato juice is tart and sour, not sweet as it should be, but I can feel my whole system soaking up the moisture like the street pavement in an early morning rain. So I take another big bite to quench my thirst.

That's when a fat brown roach crawls out of the heart of the tomato. My last bite missed him by a hair, and he's running now for his life. His tomato dinner has turned into someone else's lunch, and he doesn't want to be the main entree.

My body is soaking up the sour juice, and I can feel it giving me strength and a deep delight. This moisture is too vital. So I just pick up Mr. Roach and flip him into the cold alley. Probably out there the snowy cold will do him in. But I care only for the juice of the tomato, draining straight into my parched bloodstream. It is good, even the stem is good.

It leaves me hungry enough to crawl back up onto the Kelly green dumpster so I can look for more.

Billie Holiday only lived for two or three more years. When she died, no one told me. No one knew I even cared. In fact, at the time, I don't know that I did care, or that I even knew who she was. But she changed the course of my life that day at Carnegie.

I begged and pleaded with my Pop and finally, for my next birthday, I got a drum. A snare drum, with the stipulation I play it only outside and not bother my mother with it. Of course, I agreed. Then it took over my days and nights.

I hauled that little snare drum everywhere, beating on it all the way back and forth from school, all the way through every recess. I had a succession of little jobs, sorting pop bottles, shoveling sidewalks, delivering Chinese food, always with that snare at my side, and all of the money I made went into more and more for my kit. It kept growing, and by the time I was thirteen I had a pretty good set. Not first class, you know, but I had all the basics.

I played with brushes a lot, partly because of that night with Chico Hamilton gently driving Billie Holiday's band. But mostly because I'd drive my Mom and Dad nuts if I tried to be Buddy Rich all day long. It was a good thing, in the long run. Because of those restraints, I learned to value the swing itself and not the show. I learned that drumming was not about beating on tom-toms and crashing cymbals, it was elegantly driving the time, the time you kept, steady and irresistible. And it was using colors and notes from off the kit to line up the swing. Krupa and Rich had it all wrong. It wasn't about solos. It was my man Chico all the way. Keeping time.

I saw Billie Holiday's picture in the paper when she died, just a few years later, and that was when I really recognized who she was. But the funny thing was this, that picture didn't look like the beautiful woman who was so tired and fearful that instinctively I reached out and held her hand that night years before. I recognized her, it was definitely Lady Day, but it was almost despite her picture.

At that age, about twelve or thirteen, I started to collect photographs of her. I collected them for years, before there were any fancy photo books about Jazz, or about Ms. Holiday. Trimmed from newspapers and magazines, from articles and advertisements, I kept every photograph I could find in a little folder hidden underneath my bass drum. I can't say why, even now when I'm as normal as a Mail Box clerk can be, I can't say why I did that. It's just that I never found a picture of her, in all those years, that looked like the woman who held my hand. She was a chameleon, you know? Every photo of her looks like it was taken of a different woman, even though every picture was Billie Holiday. And I never could find a photo of the Billie Holiday I knew. Beautiful. Stately. Desperate. I never found it, though I looked for years and years. I suppose in some way I'm still looking.

She'd have been great on a police line, you know. Or as a street person, man, beautiful and invisible. What we all want.

But how do you capture the soul of a chameleon?

Now the edge of the dumpster presses into my gut as I lean over into it again. But I feel stronger. Just the juice of a couple tomatoes and some lettuce, and I feel warmer, though the snow still flurries around me. My body believes it might make it again, it might carry me through another night. It might be able to run again, to stay ahead of the noise.

"Auy," a voice from somewhere in all the noise yells. "Git ut e thire." I straighten up a little, and that lifts me from the dumpster. I can see in the dim light inside it, there is bread down at the bottom, against one wall. I lean forward so I can reach for it; the hunger for it rises.

The footsteps run up behind me, but I'm focused on the bread, the broken buns at the bottom of the dumpster. "Whet eri auy duang?" he yells at me. Then he grabs an edge of the dumpster and shoves it.

One of the heavy lids falls down and lands squarely on my back. It doesn't really hurt, though, because most of its force lands on my shoulder, and it just pushes me down inside the big can. I pitch head first into the garbage, and struggle around because it is like I'm swimming to stay above the rotting food. My feet are still tangled up with the lid and the edge of the dumpster. The only way I get free is to just stop trying to swim and dive down into the rubbery ketchup, soured pickles, liquefying lettuce moldering with the paper napkins and plastic straws. Once I dive in, my feet follow me into the dumpster, and I get them under me and come up on the other side.

A gray rat, about the size of a grapefruit, scurries up the wall of the dumpster somehow. It's amazing, the way that thing can move, scrambling right up the metal wall. I guess I am disturbing its dinner, maybe its home. In the time it takes for my eyes to spot it, the rat has squeezed itself out, barely lifting the lid. "Iglih," I hear the guy outside yell, as the rat disappears from its dumpster house, where I've been diving around. Two shafts of gray light fall down onto the green walls, pasted over with dried mustard and bluing relish smeared in streaks down from the lip of the dumpster, holding fuzzy pickle slices firmly in place.

With my feet under me, I stand up straight and shove both of the lids back. I pop up like some great jack-in-the-box and glare right at this stranger. "What's with you?" I yell at him. "Can't you just leave me the fuck alone?"

The words taste funny in my mouth, and I realize I haven't spoken to anyone in years. Years and years I think. But I don't really know how long the whispering has gone on. My mouth and my lips and my breath itself, they haven't moved like that for as long as I can remember. "Just leave me alone," I say quietly. I'm amazed really at the sounds coming from my own mouth.

But the look on his face tells me he doesn't understand. "Vygs?" he mutters, staring at me. He's wearing some brown and white polyester uniform, and a goofy little paper hat. It makes me laugh to see that paper hat.

Some ketchup and bread is stuck in my beard and I try to wipe it off with my sleeve. It just smears against my cheek, along with other stuff on my sleeve. I can smell the sweetness of it, the sugars in it all turning the fats rich and rancid. "Just leave me alone," I almost whisper to him now. The words make little or no sense in my mouth. They feel like rich, too rich creamy butter rolling on my tongue. It's like trying to speak with my mouth stuffed full of some soft cheese, but I know all to well my mouth is empty.

"Aiy'ra fockeng crizu," the guy in the funny uniform says. Then he pushes at the dumpster again and yells, "Gi un! Gat iut if hare!" He waves both hands at me, too shoo me away. "E'll cull thaa pileese!" he says.

It's no use trying to tell him anything. He can't hear me. And he looks too funny in that paper hat, talking in all the noise and not making sense. So I just pick up half of a bun from the trash, wipe it on my jeans, and then I crawl out. It takes some doing to keep that bread clean, and finally I have to hold it in my mouth and use both my hands to shimmy out of the dumpster. How did the rat climb out so easily? My feet slip out from under me, and I wind up scrambling. The dumpster rumbles like a tom tom with my footsteps scuffling up its slimy steel walls.

When I jump outside onto the gravel and broken asphalt of the alley, the little guy in the paper hat scampers back a couple of steps. With the bread still stuffed in my mouth, I raise my hands and charge at him. I make a grunting noise like a pig. He just turns and runs for a back door in the alley. As he goes, the little paper cone that he's wearing tips back, then lifts up from his head like a kite on a string. The back door slams shut behind him, and I walk over, chewing the bread and holding the rest of the bun in my hand, and I pick the hat up from the alleyway.

That's when I hear a siren and the rumble of a motorcycle, so I put on the little guy's hat and wander off deeper into the darkening and snowy alley. I look back and see the same rat, I'm sure it's the same rat, scurrying back into his dumpster. But the lids are both open, and it only takes a moment for me to stroll back over and close down the roof on the little grapefruit rat's house, to keep the evening's snow out.

They called me J. B. in the lofts. For a while, at the start, it was Bulkowski, but that was too much of mouthful for the cats. And I think it was just a city kid thing, you know, this last name as an only name business. "Yo', Bulkowski!" So before long I was J.B. The only cats who ever called me Jan were Hemp himself, and just once Mick Burns.

When I was in the thick of that scene, I kept my kit at Hemp's place. It was in an old warehouse, and the music down there was flying all the time. Any time of day or night. There was always a player around, and always somebody ready to jam.

I don't know that we really ever practiced in those days, but we played constantly. Alone, together. Music was everything, more necessary than food and water. More constant than anything but breathing. From big, huge bands, orchestras really, all the way down to solo. We played now, and we played always.

And the older cats, like Hemp or Thornton or the Pharaoh, they would always be instructing you. Not on your instrument, man, because that was your own job. You had to put your time in on your instrument, you had to have your chops down. But Hemp or Thornton, if you had your instrument down and could read and could fly when the time came, then they'd always be challenging you with something.

Sometimes Hemp would tell me, "J. B., Muhal used to say back in Chicago to us, 'The swing isn't driving! You're driving the swing.'" And he'd be telling me that I was too caught up in keeping time, that I should let the horns or the bass ride the time so I could play counter-rhythms, against the drive of the other players.

One night, when it was just the two of us playing late, he stopped and said, "You know what Cecil said about the piano, don't you, J.B.?"

Everybody knew this one. "It's 88 little drums," I said.

"You know what that means, don't you?" he said.

I sat there and tried to think of what he wanted me to say. But I didn't know what he was getting at.

Hemp strolled over and took a stick out of my hand. He tapped the center of a cymbal and got a high bell ping out of it. He let it ring for a minute while he stepped around to the front of the kit. Then he struck the bass drum from the front, dead center, got a deep thump.

"Get it?" he said.

I still sat there dumb.

He shook his head and chuckled at me, then he said, "This set of traps you got here, J. B., this is a thousand, no, it's thousands of piano keys scattered out around you," he laughed, and then stopped and grinned at me. "Name that tune, J. B.," he said.

Then he started with the bass drum and ran up four easy notes, ending with the bell ping on the cymbal. He paused for a moment, and then played the same four notes down the scale. "Got it?" he said.

I laughed and nodded my head. "It's 'Rhythm,'" I said.

"I got rhy-thm," he sang down his scale from cymbal ping to bass thump.

"If the piano man wants to play drums, Jan," Hemp grinned, "or the horn man, or the bassist," he pronounced that word precisely in two distinct syllables. "If those cats are all playing the drums, it frees you up to sing some tunes, Jan. Right? And these," he splayed his hands out like a magician who'd just made my drum kit appear out of the air. "This is your axe, baby. You can find a million tunes nobody else knows waiting right here, only for you. Right, Jan? Waiting only for you."

So it was like that at the start, learning joyfully all the time, playing to learn so you could learn to play. And right from the beginning, Mick Burns had it. He was from the suburbs, Connecticut or Massachusetts somewhere, I think. But he wasn't from the city. He came up in some suburban high school, playing sax in pep band, and listening to records. Somehow he got hip to the real stuff, you know. It was hard to say how. But somehow he heard Ornette. Someone turned him on to Cecil. And then Mick was off.

Soon as he got out of school, he moved to the city, got a job at a record store, and started hanging with the cats who play on the scene.

I met him at the record store, when I bought a Sunny Murray lp. Mick was a tall cat, with long curly blonde air . He had a slight stoop, like he was always leaning forward. And his nose was too big, really. But those wild cascades of blonde hair sort of shrunk his nose down to fit with his face. Anyway, the girls seemed to dig it. He had this deep, deep voice and the minute he spoke, the girls didn't seem to notice that his nose almost stretched to Yonkers.

Mick and I fell in together so easily. Nobody seemed to plan it, nobody was trying to get close. We just hit it off. I think, at the beginning, we were just hearing the same stuff. The Ornette that Mick was digging was clear and beautiful to me. And I would play the Art Ensemble stuff and talk about Wilson or Moye, and Mick could hear that. We were in the same place. So naturally, we became a duo: Mick on reeds, me on drums. The bass players came and went, and there were bunches of guitarists and a whole string of all kind of horn players. But they all seemed to come and go in a stream, and the only steady thing was Mick on reeds and J.B. on drums.

We played on the streets a lot in those days. I'd just set up a snare and a cymbal, Mick and whoever else was in the band at the moment, would open up their cases for change, and away we would go.

We had gigs at some coffeehouse or pub now and then, but not many. It was mostly in the streets we played. One day Mick showed up at our agreed upon corner and just says, "J. B., c'mon." He had this bright twinkle in his eye, and he laughed happily.

Mick met this girl in the record store, Cleo as her name, I think. She took us up that afternoon to meet Hemp. I think mostly she wanted to get into Mick's pant's, and he was pretty obliging. But the big news was this lady was taking us to meet Hemp.

That was our doorway into the real world. We went to a party at Hemp's loft, we jammed with him, and we stayed. Mick and I, we just didn't really leave. We played off and on with him most of the night. Then in the early morning we all crashed. When we woke up we were still there, so we played some more.

It went on like that.

"You think you're doing what?" my father said.

He shook his head slowly, slightly, and stared at something in the floor. "I should never have let Leo take you over there."

"This has got nothing to do with Uncle Leo," I said.

"He was so proud of that job. How could I say no? He got such a kick out of showing off to you, Jan. It was such a big thing to him." My father spoke to the worn carpet by the front door, "How could I say no to him?"

My father had saved all the money he could, after years in the wallpapering business. He wanted only one thing from me, his only son: He wanted me not to be what he was, a working schmuck. He wanted a doctor or a lawyer. Not for any status. It was for safety. He'd been through immigration and then the Depression. He'd pounded the streets looking for work, he'd been tossed from one job to another. He'd scraped to get by, struggled to keep a roof over us, fought to get his family out of Poland.

But twenty years of selling wallpaper, of contracting out to hang paper, of hanging it himself when he needed to, of haggling with housewives and sales reps, had led to a little nest egg set side to give me a better start. I was supposed to be somebody. A doctor. A lawyer. It didn't matter which, but it had to be one of those two. Everything else was too insecure. "You got to get yourself a profession, Jan," he used to say. And when he said that, his eyes climbed naturally up the papered walls to gaze at something on the ceiling.

Playing drums on a street corner didn't measure up.

"This is not a profession, Jan," he said to me, frowning, the deep lines in his face creasing with pain. "This is a hobby. This is something you do on the weekend. After work."

The first blow came when I didn't go on to school. But that could always be changed. I could always start late. It was good to get some life experience behind you, before you got into the law or medicine. It could be corrected, this first "mistake" of mine.

The second blow came when I discovered I could scrape together a living, playing drums wherever I could. Understand, it wasn't really enough to rent a place of my own, but it was enough to eat and I could pay my folks some rooming money with what I brought in.

I guess my father thought it was a lever he could use to pry me loose, and get me into college. "You can't live a here all your life, Jan. You're a man now, and it's time to have a place of your own." He thought sending me out into the city to make a living would crush the music right out of me, send me running back to school.

"If you want to go to college, Jan, your mother and I will be glad to help. But until then, you need to find your own apartment," he told me, when my mother was not around.

That was the third blow, I think. He was there when Mick and some others helped me move out. I moved into Hemp's loft, and so did Mick, so we could practice all the time. Hemp didn't really suggest it. It just seemed the natural thing to move in with our teacher. Hemp had the space, we could work with him and gig with him, and his connections would set us off and running with the real cats.

So as Mick and I carried out the pieces of my kit, my Father stood and watched. "Come back when you're ready to get a real profession," he said, looking old and defeated and foreign.

"See ya'," I said. I smiled, trying to put a good face on things. But my smile only seemed defiant and nasty to him.

He stood in the doorway as we hauled the last of my stuff down the stairs. Then he yelled, "Don't be looking to me or your mother to bail you out!" He yelled that so the whole neighborhood could hear. As if it would mean something to everybody out there, as if it would shame me back to my senses.

Mick, with his family in the suburbs and his job at the record store, stood there holding a cymbal case and trying not to look back up at the Old Man, trying to disappear into the sidewalk.

"Let's get outa here," I said.

I waved to my father as he turned, scowling at the walls, and closed the door to my home.

Now the motorcycle rumble gets even louder and turns into a grating roar as the cop wheels around into the alley. I see him over the top of the rat's dumpster, but he doesn't see me. He's just answering the call. As the bike rounds the sharp corner, I duck down a little and slip between the back of the dumpster and the brick wall. I hear the rat scuffle for a moment inside the dumpster. The grapefruit rat is settling into a warm hiding place, too. He knows the cops are outside.

The cop on the bike rolls slowly down the alley, turning the front wheel from side to side to stay balanced. I see him go by, but he doesn't see me. His white helmet is turning side to side, in a motion almost counter to the weaving of his front wheel.

Then the back door opens and that kid, without his paper hat, steps out. The cop pulls up and puts one foot out to steady the bike. The kid is pointing down here toward the dumpster, and talking to the cop, but he doesn't see me in the shadows of the narrow alley. He's just pointing at the rat's dumpster and speaking to the cop.

I move a step or two down to the other side of the trash bin, to get it between me and the hatless kid. I must be the movement that does it. Probably the kid's stupid hat on my head--it's white with yellow trim--catches their eye when I move. Because suddenly the kid bolts a couple steps toward me. "Hud, thuri os!" he yells.

The cop starts to turn his fat bike around. I slip out to the other side of the dumpster, my hands pressing against the cool metal wall of it. "Thuri os!" I hear the kid yell again. Then the bike revs up to a roar and I hear it shooting back down toward me.

I just turn and run, and in a moment I'm out of the alley and running down the sidewalk. As I turn the corner, at a full sprint, I crash right into some young guy in a suit and a soft brown overcoat. He goes right down onto the sidewalk with me and I land on top of him, but I catch my weight in my hands.

There's a moment then where I see straight into the brown overcoat's eyes. They're green, and the pupils are all dilated. His face is frozen in this contorted grimace, with his mouth open. When I look in his eyes--he's just a young guy in a white shirt and a neck tie--but he thinks he's going to die right there and then. He says, "Ageh, dogeh, gogedh," and there is some spit coming out of the corner of his open mouth.

The roar of the motorcycle behind me cuts to a rattle. Then I hear the cop yelling at me, "Stam! Stam, yu! Stam!"

I glance over my shoulder and see the cop down at the entrance to the alley. He's setting the kickstand on his bike. Then the hatless kid bursts out of the alley and comes to a halt behind the cop's bike. The brown overcoat underneath me is still drooling and talking nonsense.

"You're all right," I yell down at him, and in a yell so loud I can feel the paper hat on my head shift forward a little, "Nobody's gonna hurt you." But he doesn't understand a word I say. He just sucks up the drool in his mouth and he starts shaking. I could yell at him some more, I feel 1 like it, but what good would it do? He can't understand me anyway.

I hear the cop, with the kid right behind him, running toward me. But it doesn't matter, because I'm fast as the wind. I rise up off of that brown overcoat still trembling on the cold concrete and I run faster than anybody can, because I don't care if I knock people down, I don't care if the taxis must stomp on their brakes, I don't care if people yell at me and cars blow their horns, I don't care if some messenger boy wrecks his bike and dumps all the precious little messages out into the streets, I don't care if a tall delivery truck runs right into me. I don't care. I only care that I'm running. And all the noise is gone again. All the whispering. Gone.

"Sta! Sta!" I hear the cop yelling. But he disappears back into the suits and the overcoats and the hot little red and purple jackets standing all along the street, parting in front of me like rainbows reflected in water, like an oil slick riding under a speedboat.

And I am that speedboat.   Roaring louder than all the noise around me.

These days I call my father every Sunday, back in Brooklyn. He likes to complain about work, about overtime and short vacations and lost weekends, and back to work on Monday. This job of mine at the Mail Box, he understands this. This to him is work. Drudgery, the boredom of it, something to hate every morning, traveling to work in that long procession that leads in the end, really, to your funeral. This, for my father, is a job. Not playing music

But I'm being too hard. I know deep in my heart this is the job he wanted to save me from. All those dreams and plans about a profession, all that talk about law school and med school, it was all meant to save me from this: Day after day, smiling through the boredom, sweeping up the paper and the styrofoam at the store's close, heading for the commute. This was what he meant to save me from.

But he's wrong. I know that now; I learned it on my own, on the streets of the city. Whether I was playing a kit or sleeping on some step, I learned it out there on the city sidewalks, just around the corner from the alleys where the dumpsters waited. My father is wrong. It's not like that.

"Good night, Johnny," Bernie said, "See you in the morning."

I was pushing the broom around in the back room. With all the packing and stuffing that goes on during the day there, it gets to be quite the mess at the Mail Box. So every night, after the doors are closed and the front lights are down, I sweep up.

In the back room, by the gate where the UPS truck comes, is my favorite spot. There is an expanse of concrete floor there, and after we've loaded the day's stuff onto UPS, the room can be pretty empty. This is the time of day when the back room has a nice echo to it.

"You drive safe now, Bernie," I said. Then she locked the door behind me, and I'm alone for a minute in back.

When the broom hits the concrete floor it creates a "barroo-oo-shsh" sound. It's all in the attack. "Barrooshsh," it goes. "Barrooshsh." Every third time, I let it bounce a bit to get a "barr-barr-oosh." I hear a triplet inside a the 4/4 time of the sweeping. Sweep, sweep, sweep, and then " barr-barr-oosh-oosh." The beat echoes around the empty back room.

It felt good that night, just like it did that slow afternoon when I built my cardboard kit back there. It is a trance, in a way, I can fall into, inside the time, so all I'm doing is that triplet on the fourth beat. I'm not sweeping, I'm not cleaning up. I'm not even at the Mail Box. I'm just keeping time.

It is the place you get to, behind the kit, when you can start to play free. The beat is so deep inside, you don't even feel it anymore. It is just everywhere, holding up reality itself, so now you're free to play whatever you can create. You're no longer keeping time. The time is keeping you.

I pulled up the broom and stopped. I told myself it was only Thursday night. I still had to get through Friday and Saturday before I reached my days off. I had to be here first thing in the morning to cover the register up front. Early to clean the windows, too. The floor looked good, good enough. Not spotless, but good enough to pass Bernie's muster in the morning.

I set the broom in the corner and put on my coat. It was raining and I could hear the random rhythm of the raindrops on the cheap metal roof over my head. But I didn't let it fall into any kind of beat.

I got the hell out because I had some more long days to the week ahead. I was beat.

But I knew my father would be proud.

That way perdition lies.

"Hey, J.B." Mick Burns held up a dark green bottle, "Check this out."

It was a bottle of wine, Chardonnay it said, and not some jug wine. It came from some small vineyard upstate. "Whoa, Mick!" I said. "I don't know crap about wine. But that looks like it must have cost some change. This don't say Gallo on it anywhere."

"J. B., that bottle would cost you a couple Franklins midtown." Mick carefully set the bottle at the back of the refrigerator, behind all the milk bottles and half empty Chinese food cartons. "Rebecca is gonna love this," he said. Rebecca was this girl who worked at the store with Mick. She had raven black hair that tumbled in the air with a life of its own. He'd been trying to get in her pants since the day she started.

"Where'd you get the cash for something like that?" I said.

"It's this cat who comes in the store, man," Mick said. "He makes the stuff. Only sells it to restaurants, you know. But I'm always helping him find some interesting records, turning him on to stuff he wouldn't hear otherwise. He's a god cat.

"Today when he comes in, he says, 'I heard you last night, man. Out on the street corner, you were playing some great, crazy stuff.' Then he hands me this bottle of wine. He goes, 'I enjoyed your stuff for free, now you should enjoy some of my stuff. Right?' What a beautiful cat, huh?" Mick turned the bottle a little in the refrigerator, so the label was up and he could admire it.

"Wait a minute, Mick," I said. "I played that gig on the street with you, last night. Right?"

Mick was closing the door to the fridge, and he said, "So? The cat told me I had some lame ass drummer on the date." He laughed.

"Shit," I said. I put my hand on the handle of the fridge, "I deserve some of that fancy Chardonnay, too! Let's try it out, Mick."

I figured then that he just wanted to get in this Rebecca's jeans. It never crossed my mind there might be more going on than that. "No, J. B.," he said, with a flat stern stare, "I'm saving that bottle." He glared first at my hand on the refrigerator door, and then at my face.

"Leave that bottle alone, J. B.," he said. "It belongs to me."

"All right, all right," I said. "Lighten up, Mick. Man, I was just joking around." But somehow, it was all different between us after that moment. Everything had changed.

People think drugs, you know. They see some person out on the street, and they don't think of confusion, they don't think of poverty, they don't think illness. They don't think of lost dreams and broken hearts. They think drugs.

People don't care whether it's heroin, crack or juice, or whatever. It's all the same to them. It's all drugs. And why else, they ask themselves, would a person be out here in that condition on the street? It has to be drugs. And the madness that comes from them. It has to be. These are lost people who just didn't have the gumption to say no. Right?

This is the way people walking by you think, when you're sleeping on the stoop or hiding in the alley, chasing the rats out of a good dumpster.

But I have to tell you: I was clean. I'm clean now. I was clean when I heard Billie Holiday sing and Chico Hamilton play. I was clean when I played the street corners with Mick Burns. And I was clean when I ran on those streets, when no one could understand a word that I said, not the police, not the fast food jerks, not the suits and ties strolling the ave. Nobody could speak clearly. Nobody could hear me. But I was clean, clean as the morning of my birth, maybe cleaner than ever before. I was sparkling once, and in the streets I was burning lean and hard as granite. Time rolled over me like a boulder, but I couldn't fracture because I was dense and tough and uncrushable. I was a rock, harder and clearer and just as alone as a diamond. But no one knew.

Because they all knew it was drugs that put me there. But they weren't even close. See, the only drug that ever spoke to me was the sound of Billie Holiday, singing a subtle variation on an old melody. That's the only drug I ever knew.

And that way perdition lies.

Hemp wasn't clean though. No needles, no snort. But if it came in a bottle, Hemp loved it dearly and spent part of every day with it. As much of every day with it as he could. He was never drunk, though. It never touched his playing, or his composing. Or at least not that anyone could tell.

I've seen Hemp up there in that room of his, horn in his hands, three in the morning, with a bottle of gin half empty on the chair beside him, and another bottle, empty, at his feet. And he'd clearly say, without a touch of a slur, "This is 'The Hard Blues,' J. B." Then he'd plant his feet and play that alto, with his eyes open and looking at the sheet of music propped up on the chair beside his second bottle of gin. He'd run through some crazy kind of melody, and it was hard to hear the changes, and you'd swear he was just flying, improvising, out of his mind. Wild, but beautiful.

Then he'd come to the end, shake his head at something he wasn't happy with. He'd pick up a pencil and scratch a few marks on the paper. I'd feel like saying, "Hemp, baby, we should've had a tape running. You'll never catch a solo like that again." But I'd learned from a string of nights like this to keep my mouth shut. Because he'd say, once he'd set the pencil down and held the gin bottle in his hand, "I can't get this quite right, J. B. And this must be the twentieth draft." Then he'd plant his feet and take that alto up and play it all again, almost note for note, except for the little changes he'd made. It was all written down. And he was playing it tight, over and over and over again. Until the gin was gone.

Then we'd eat, and he'd sleep until noon, or later.

So he wasn't clean, not when there was something to drink around. And I don't know now what Mick Burns was thinking. But it may have had more to do with me than with the wine and with Rebecca.

"They signed him, man," Hemp smiled wistfully at the floor. "Did you hear that? Mick just signed up with a big ass record company, J. B. They're gonna give him the big blow." Then Hemp laughed, and there was the touch of bitterness in it, the jaded sound of experience. "Better watch out, J. B. You all gonna get the big blow."

It was noon and Hemp was just up. He was spiking juice with a bit of gin, rubbing his eyes, waking up for the day. "What?" I asked, trying to be careful. I didn't want to believe something too good to be true. "What happened to Mick?"

Hemp chuckled again, took a long swallow of his spiked orange juice. "It's happened to you too, little drummer boy."

"Slow down, Hemp. What's going on? I don't want to get all hopped up about nothing," I said.

He shook his head, then he looked deep into my eyes and said, "Be careful, little J. B. Don't let them mess with your head. They only want you cats because you're young and you got pretty young faces. When you don't make them a million dollars, and you won't make them their million dollars, then they'll throw you away. So don't let it go to your head, J. B. Don't believe them, whatever they tell you. Because pretty soon, sooner than you think, you're gonna be just another old cat at the drums."

"Hemp, what are you talking about?"

"They just want your pretty face up on their record jacket, Jan."

"Record jacket?"

Hemp tilted his head back and drained the juice glass. Then he sat for a moment, licking his lips. As he began to make another juice and gin, this one with less of the juice, he said as if he spoke to the glass, "Some record exec heard you cats at that late night cafe gig, and he signed Mick. Columbia, man," Hemp blew a high pitched whistle at that. "Mick signed a two record deal with Columbia."

"Columbia," I said.

"Don't let it hit you, J. B. Don't count on nothing from them. Remember. This is the company that screwed with Ornette. And they ruined Arthur, little drummer man. Had him playing pretty with strings and shit. Sounding like Al Hirt or some god damned thing. Then they threw the brother away. These are the people, Jan, they threw Ornette away." Hemp spoke with a pinched voice and he squinted his eyes, as if it hurt to say it out loud. "They'll throw you away, too. Watch your head through all this shit, J. B. They'll either twist your head or screw your ass. One or the other, if not both, if you let 'em. If you let 'em, they'll steal your heart, Jan. They'll take your art away from you and prostitute it on the street corners of their two-bit towns. Don't let 'em, Jan." He stopped and took another swallow. "Don't let 'em," he nearly whispered.

But I was young and stupid then. I thought I knew myself, knew what I was about, what I was driving toward. I told myself, What does Hemp know? He's recorded a lot, done a lot. But he never had no Columbia records signing him up, never the big time. It was always little one shot record companies, some cat storing records in his mother's basement, getting his girlfriend to do the cover art, and then going broke. Or some European label, that cost a firstborn child to buy and no record store could ever find. These are the people who made Hemp's records. They were great, but nobody ever heard them. Nobody had ever heard them. So what did Hemp know, with his gin and his Italian record deals? This is what I told myself. What did Hemp know about any big time Columbia records?

Hemp was just jealous. Jealous and drunk.

This is what I told myself as I went through that door that led me out onto the street. This is what I knew. What I knew back then.

But it's what you don't know that'll bite you in the ass.

Now the suits and ties seem to part in front of me. I fly down the sidewalk. Block after block rolls by. Cracks in the sidewalk curl beneath my feet. The lights are red, the lights are green, the lights show me that little person walking, the lights show me a burning hand up in the air. Burning so bright it spoke to me. Run, run, the burning light said.

So I fly. I lift up right off the ground and into the air. They yell more noise at me, yabber-yabber-yabbering at me, and car horns blow in the air. But the suits and the furs all part before me and I fly on the ground between them. I fly, until the police are all gone. Just cabs and cars, and no burger jerks or motorcycle cops to haunt me.

"Luck ut!" some of the suits yell to the furs, and pull them aside. Out of my flying way. "His crezz," they yell. "Luck ut!" I see their frightened faces all in a row, but they blur together as I run until I don't see them anymore. I only see coats and crazy neckties and stringed beads dangling from their ears.

My chest begins to ache then, all the cold air pumping in and out of me. I run into the alley, but the alley is different. I stop just around the corner from the street, just out of sight of all the people out there, yabbering and yabbering. The twilight has fallen down into night now. I stand, propped against a brick wall, and pant in the bitter cold. The air is too brittle and frozen to breathe; it hurts my lungs to breathe it so deeply. But the shallow breaths that would keep me warm can't fill my lungs now.

I am warm, I'm even sweating around the collar of my sweatshirt, but my lungs keep pulling in the frigid night air. With each tug of my breath, I pull the cold inside of myself deeper. But I can't help it. I want to stop breathing and huddle inside the warmth in my belly, but I need the air. I need it, though it's cold chips away at my warmth with every pant like an ice pick.

But this alleyway is different. I've crawled through a thousand black streets in this last long day, punctuated by a hundred nights huddled in a hundred alleys, all of them the same long alleyway, peopled with rats and fat roaches and grinding hydraulic trucks creeping along, swallowing everything they touch. But this alley is different.

The cold and the snow are cutting through me. I walk down the narrow brick alley, understanding somehow where I'm going. I don't remember anything, only the cold and the steel snow coming at me, but I know if I walk down here and turn right at the end, in front of the brick wall, that underneath an iron fire escape, I will find the stage door. It won't be locked at this time of night. The taxis and limos will pull up from the other direction, and the stars will fly in and out of that little door.

My body is drawn there. I don't remember anything, but I know the warmth that will flow out of that stage door, and out of those heated town cars. Gusts of warmth will well out onto the cold alley, and so my body drags me there, like a speckled moth drawn to the heat and the light of a candle flame.

I can't say how, there is no memory in my bones, but I know the warmth of that stage door is waiting for me there. It is painted dark green, with white letters stenciled across it, but I can't make any sense of them. I sit down in the alley beside the door, right alongside it and I look down at the dirty street. No one would see me. I'll become just another piece of refuse lying amidst the brick and asphalt, more dirt heaped into the worn corners of the ancient street.

I was right. First it is a town car pulls up, but I keep my head down and don't look at it. I stare at the hard snow swirling around my feet, brightened in the headlights of the car, filling the crevices in the old pavement. My body waits for the wave of warmth, and it comes. First a little wave of heat as the car doors open, and then a wonderful gust of warmth as the big green door is held open. "Kerfil," a man says, and his legs step between me and the heat rolling from beyond the green door. I don't look up, because he's not speaking to me, he's speaking to whoever is stepping inside the building.

I push my face down lower, into the knees of my pants. Inside I hear the voices, snapping back and forth at one another, and in the distance, another, deeper voice. A man's voice, speaking slowly. Amplified. Echoing around the warmth inside the building. Heat from the doorway flows around me, carrying that warm, familiar voice with it.

Then, for the first time really, I hear it.

Mick Burns seemed entirely calm. He sat in the big overstuffed chair in Hemp's loft, gazing at the arch his fingertips made as he pressed them together. "Jan," he said quietly, "I'm gonna be making some changes."

He was sitting there when I burst in. He didn't seem startled. In fact, I think now he was waiting for me. "Mick," I said, "Hemp told me."

He paused and looked up at me from his fingertips. "Told you what?" he said.

"About the record deal," I said, and grinned with my own excitement. "It's great, isn't it?"

Mick looked back at his hands, but only for moment.

"Have you decided what we should put down, Mick?" I said. "That blues with the inversion half way through, that'd make great opening cut, don't you think? We could use it at the end too. That one always got a lot of tips in the street, so . . ."

He stood up quietly. He looked about twenty years older than me then, and about twelve feet tall. He didn't have to ask me to be quiet. I just stopped, and then he looked straight at me and said, "I'm gonna make some changes, Jan. The line up is changing now." He walked over to me, put a hand on my shoulder and said, "I'm gonna be using a different drummer." His voice sounded as deep and as serious as my father's.

Then Mick turned and walked out of the loft. As an after thought, he looked back from the doorway and said, "Jan? Thanks, man. Thanks for hanging in there." Then he disappeared through that doorway.

Sometimes, when Bernie leaves at night, and I'm in the back here sweeping up, she says from the doorway, "Thanks, Johnny." It echoes through the empty Mail Box and I sweep it away with the strokes of my broom.

She means it though. Bernie is on the way to the top of the Mail Box. Regional Manager, Head

Office. All that stuff. Unless the UPS steals her away. When I do my job, it makes her look good, and she is headed for the top. The top of the Mail Box ladder to success. Road to that big UPS delivery door in the sky. So she means it when she says, "Thanks, Johnny," at night, just before the door closes behind her. Even if she can't get my name right.

What she doesn't know is that it still makes the floor quake beneath my feet. I sweep harder than ever, because I'm sweeping away the street.

Now I recognize the deep, woody tone of his chalumeau, gliding through that open green door. It cuts through all the confusion around me, and I recognize it. Immediately. It isn't his voice speaking, all the voices speaking, all the voices speaking at me, it is that tone. Dark, deep, woody. Like no one else.

Then it stops, and I hear the scattering voices around me from just inside the green door. The suit that just went inside comes back out and stands over me. I don't look up but I see the worn shoes he wears. They've traveled a lot of distance, but they shine. They're polished and clean, old but buffed up to a high shine. "Rot hir, bid. Rot ba da durwhy," he says to someone back inside the door.

Then I hear it again, that woody chalumeau. I lift my head and glance back inside, where it is coming from. That tone is the first thing in my whole life, at that moment, the only thing I can remember as far back as I can go, the first thing that makes any sense. It's not just sounds, not confused yelling. I know it.

"Bedda muv on, bod," the suit says to me. "Bifur dey cull da cops." I look at his face, he's just a young guy in a snazzy uniform with a tie and a cap and I realize he's the driver. That's all. He's just the driver and he's trying to help me out. It's the people he drives around who are after me, who have disappeared back inside toward that blackened, woody tone.

The driver pulls a buck out of his pocket and hands it to me, "Ooo luck bad, body," he says. I gaze up at his eyes and he sees into me. I hear that singing tone behind him, through the green door. "Git ursilf sumthan to eek," he says, as I reach up to take the bill he's handing me.

The tone begins to sing, to rise up from the low chalumeau and squeal. It begins to croon a tune I know, and I stand up with the driver's dollar bill in my hand. He takes a couple steps back, away from me and he says, "Bedda git oota hir, body." But I'm only hearing that melody now, playing on his clarinet. "Thir culling thi cops," the driver says to me.

He is not just playing the melody. His clarinet is scraping and squealing around it, adding noise to the notes. This is why I can hear it, I think, this is why it speaks to me, because it's not just a pretty melody, it's not just a song in the air, it's not just a dollar bill in the hand. It is a string of beautiful notes struggling to emerge from the noise all around it.   But me, I am hearing so much noise all the time that this makes sense.   If he'd played just the tune, it would have been lost.   Buried under the noise, lost in all the yelling and screaming I hear, all the time.   I would never hear it.   But to pull that song, that beautiful song, out of all the noise in this world, this is what lets me hear him.

I push my way in, through the big green door, because I know him.   I know who it is.   I know his tone, I know his clarinet, and now, for the first time in my life, ever, I know his song.

I was so stunned I didn't know what to say to Mick, he was gone out the door and I was still back somewhere hearing him say, "I'm gonna be making some changes, J. B."

But in a moment I shoved my way through the door and ran out of Hemp's loft. Mick was already gone, the open stair was empty.   It clattered noisily as I ran down, taking two or three steps at a time.   I kept telling myself that I must have heard him wrong.   He couldn't be meaning what I think he said, that I was gone.

There was a heavy metal door that opened out onto the street.   It didn't have a knob, but an aluminum bar that I pushed and the door swung out onto a side alley.   I ran and it seemed I just touched that bar and the door flung me out onto the streets. There was a short alley, and I saw Mick burns turn to his left and walk away.   There was an urgency to his step, and I wondered if losing me was that urgency. "Mick," I yelled, but he didn't look back.

I ran after him, and now I felt my own confusion behind me. There was a coterie of voices speaking to me, just behind my head. But no matter how quickly I turned around, I could never find anyone. Even if I jerked my head to look back, just a glance really. But nobody was ever there. "Hey, Mick," I yelled, and caught up to him on the hustling sidewalk. He didn't stop his steady stride down the street, and people were crossing us and passing by and in front of us, and they all seemed to be muttering, just little too low to be heard.

"Mick?" I said, as he looked blankly at me but didn't stop walking. I was panting, and that's when I realized that what I thought I'd heard him say was true. I was not on the date. I didn't get the gig. I was gone. I was left behind, and only this urgent muttering was left, nipping at my heels. "Mick, why?" I said, because I didn't know what else to say. Because I didn't know why.

At first Mick Burns looked tired. He took a deep breath. But then something passed over him, like the shadow of a bird, and he stopped on the sidewalk and looked straight and unblinking into my eyes. But the people around us didn't stop. In fact, they seemed to hurry more, as if the shadow that had passed over Mick and I had frightened them. "I'm sorry, J. B." Mick said.

"But?"

He glanced down at the sidewalk, and then he looked up and straight into my eyes again. "You just can't cut it, Jan. You can't keep up."

I couldn't look back at him anymore. My gaze fell down to the sidewalk until only the hard concrete felt real. All the people hurrying by out there, they all began to speak to me at once. It took all my concentration to cut through them and hear what Mick said. His voice sounded thinner and it was sliding away from me, into the street. But I heard him say, "We just need someone who can do more, Jan." Then he paused as if he was looking for something more to say to me. When no more words came, Mick Burns shook his head no, and then he walked away. I stood, gazing down at the sidewalk, listening, filled with shame. The street around me was humming with voices.

Chico had his brush on the snare and he rode the high hat softly. Just a shoosh, shoosh, shoosh behind her as she sang. Her voice had a rasp, and it searched to hold the key, but she sang so it cut into you like a razor. That night was the first time I ever heard "Lady Sings the Blues."

It is what his clarinet sings now. "Lady Sings the Blues." I recognize the tune. I can hum along. I can remember Chico Hamilton riding behind Lady herself on that night long ago. Way back at the beginning of my life.

Now I am seven years old again, I can almost hear the Lady singing. And in the background I can hear the roar, the loud jumble of words, the shouts and howls, they are beginning to sort themselves out. Because the sound of that clarinet is piercing now, with its squawks and yells, it is piercing through the noise all around me.

So I begin to recognize all this noise I am hearing all the time. And, because I can hear that song squealing from his clarinet, I know that my roar is made up of voices. But now they are beginning to come apart, to stop roaring and shouting and become a battery of separate voices, calling and demanding and yelling to me all at once.

I step in through the big green door, drawn by the song of the clarinet. There is still a jumble of voices, yelling about me, but now they are voices with a clarinet singing above them, singing the blues. Singing for the Lady. There are hands placed on me, all around me, but I don't struggle and I don't run, because I can hear him playing his clarinet for Lady Day.

I just stand in the old doorway listening, and the roar all around me becomes slowly just a confusion of voices.

Then an old man with tears in his eyes puts an arm around me. He holds my shoulder and he leads me farther into the room. I know him. I know him from long ago, and I know he won't try to hold me or pen me up. I am afraid, I realize, that if someone pens me up or holds me too still for too long, then the roar all around me, the noise of the crashing down world, the constant rattling without any rhythm or song, it might sweep over me. Then it might envelope me. Then I will be swallowed up.

But I know this old man won't hold me. I know he will let me run, if I need to run. And besides, there is the sound of the clarinet. The singing above the voices.

Uncle Leo leads me over toward the stage, and I am standing in the wings, the way I did when I was seven years old. Uncle Leo keeps an arm around my shoulder and he steadies me, and the clarinet cuts through the confusion of calling larks circling around my head.

Out on the stage, he stops playing and begins to speak. In a soft voice he tells the audience about the beauty of folk songs, the wealth of imagination that belongs to us all because it came from us all, but it is overlooked in all of its complexity, thought only to be simple. Then he plays again, and the sound of his clarinet is deep and wooden and familiar. It is dark wood. It is playing inside my head, and now I know it has been playing inside my head since before I was born.

His music makes me tremble, and I lean over into Uncle Leo. The clarinet stops again and he begins to speak. I look out at him on the stage, at his gray curly hair, at the way he lightly stoops forward, I hear his warm resonant voice, deep and woody as his clarinet.

I remember now that I played with him. We played together once, long ago it seems, in the loft where Hemp lived. I remember his warm voice, the depth of what he played, the way Hemp smiled back at me when I touched the cymbals at the tastiest moment, the way he spoke to me after we played. With his clarinet in his hand, and with Hemp listening, he thanked me. He thanked me for playing so well.

"Jan," Uncle Leo says. "Jan, are you all right?"

Hemp was sitting in the kitchen at the table when he said it. His hand rested on the tabletop, and he sipped now and then from a little glass filled with red wine. The bottle, two-thirds gone, sat in front of him.

"That bottle that was in there night before last," he said as I walked in, "was that yours, J. B.?"

I had been out walking around, trying to understand the news. Mick Burns had just dropped me from the band. Our big break had come, and I was left out. After we talked in the street, I spent the afternoon walking around the city trying to understand. "You can't cut it," Burns had said. "I need someone who can keep up," he had said.

Hemp took another sip from the juice glass in his hand. "Was that yours, J. B.?" he said, and then he grinned.

I wanted to tell him about Mick Burns, about the way I'd been left behind. But I couldn't decide what to say. There were too many words coming at me, trying to explain it all. "You can't cut it," Mick had said, and I couldn't get those words out of my head. "I need someone who can keep up."

"What?" I said to Hemp

"That was a nice little bottle of wine, man," Hemp said. "That was some fine, fine stuff, J.B. I'm sorry you missed it, but I promise you I'll get another one for you, J. B. I'll get you better than that. I know this sweet little port, brown as a ripe berry. I'll get you a bottle of that port, okay? To make up for that wine of yours I drank."

He was always saying things like that, telling you he would buy you a drink. But it always seemed like when the bar tab came, Hemp was gone. He'd catch it next time, he'd say. Over and over. Always next time.

"What bottle of wine?" I said.

"The one that was in the fridge night before last," Hemp said.

I realized then he was talking about Mick's bottle, the fancy wine Mick got as a tip. The bottle Mick was planning to use to peel off Rebecca's hot pants. Hemp had drunk Mick Burn's big night away, stolen it right out of the refrigerator.

"It was some good stuff," Hemp said. "For white, it was damn fine. You got good taste in wine, J. B."

"You drank that bottle of wine?" I said. The thought resonated through me like the sound of a bell. "The bottle of Chardonnay that was in the fridge?"

Hemp gave me this little grin of his, then he took another sip of his juice glass. He was going to change the subject. He was about to talk about music, about who we might be playing with over the weekend, or about the structure of some Ornette tune, or the night he played with Max Roach. About anything other than the wine, or for that matter the port he'd just promised me.

"Shit," I said, "that's it." I turned back to the door, trying to remember where Mick was headed when he left. "I gotta find Mick," I said.

"Don't be pissed off about the wine, man," Hemp said. I heard him as I went out the door. "Don't be pissed off, J. B." he whined. But I ran down the stairs and out onto the streets again. I had to find him, I had to explain to him what happened. But I didn't know where Mick Burns had gone.

Running down the streets of the Village looking for him, I kept hearing Hemp saying, "Don't be pissed off, J B." It was louder than the voice of Mick Burns repeating, "I need someone who can cut it," over and over in my ears.

And now finally he begins to play the blues on his clarinet, straight and simple and slow. "Nobody knows" and "Motherless Child," and out of the notes he builds it up to a great mountain of sadness and heartbreak and then he lets the squeaks and cries and the noise of the black wood wash over the top of it all, wash it down until it drains away, and he is alone, and motionless, and strong, standing before us on the stage, and everything and everyone else is silent. And the voices are silent. And I am alone in the quiet of his horn.

Then came the applause.

"Jan," Uncle Leo said, "come with me." Uncle Leo led me down a narrow hallway backstage to a bathroom. He mopped at the tears on his face with his fingers, and he sniffed now and again as he repeated my name. Inside Leo stood next to me in front of the mirror, under the bright, bare lights. And I saw myself.

I was wearing a paper hat from that burger joint on the back of my head. It was tilted off to one side so it covered one of my ears and barely reached the top of my head. The elastic string that held the hat in place was not around or under my chin, it was just tangled in my hair.

And my hair was matted in one flattened ball around my face. On the side of my head, opposite the paper burger hat, a tongue of hair the size and color of a big rotten carrot shot straight out. It was like a ponytail that had climbed around to rest in my other ear.

I reached up to touch that carrot of hair—-it was stiff and dry as a wad of steel wool, but so brittle some of it broke off at my touch—-and I saw the back of my hand.

The gray, sooty grime was rubbed into my skin, some of it oily, some of it dry and crusted. Only the tips of my fingers and the heels of my palms were clean. I turned my hand around, examining it. The nails were long and black, broken and cracked where they hadn't split. When I closed my fist, I could see the worn, white cracks of my knuckles protrude from the oily gray, like little white-bellied fish rising to feed in a slick.

The applause ended then. The beautiful whine of the clarinet sang out again. It cut through the air, as I looked at my face in the mirror, and he played every song I'd ever known on his clarinet, all at once. All of music came back to me at once, in a flood. The tears slid down my oily, pocked cheeks and into the matted hair on my face. There were pieces of hamburger bun and things I couldn't recognize knit into my beard. But it didn't matter, because I could hear again. He was playing "God Bless the Child."

Uncle Leo walked over and opened a little drawer. He handed me a bar of soap and a washrag. Then he leaned over and turned on the hot water. He put his hand on the filthy shoulder of my coat. Gently he patted my back, he didn't squeeze my shoulder, he just rested his hand there and waited for me.

I stuck my hands under the water and began to wash away the grime. Weeks, months, years of grime. I had no idea which. "I'll go get some clean clothes, Jan," he said, wiping at one of his eyes with the back of his hand.

The hot water ran over and through my fingers, and the song of the clarinet mixed with the hiss of the faucet. "Thank you," I looked at my Uncle in the mirror, and then I said his name. "Uncle Leo." It was so simple and clear. It amazed even me, because the words still felt like stones rolling around on my tongue. But I said them clearly and he understood, and I felt like the clarinet had drawn me back into a community, lured me back onto the rocky shores of life.

"Uncle Leo?" I asked, staring at my own apparition in the mirror. I reached up and pulled the paper hat off my head and held it in my hand. I swallowed once, to move my tongue around. I was afraid that what I had to say might disappear again into the noise of all the voices. "Uncle Leo," I asked, "how did you know it was me?"

A smile broke across his lips in the mirror. "It was the clarinet, Jan," he said. "I saw the way you heard him play, the way you sat up and turned your head." Then he laughed. "It had to be you," he said.

The moment he opened the door to the washroom, the song of the clarinet welled up louder and clearer. "God bless the child," it sang, "who's got his own." Then the door swung shut and muffled the tone again.

Mick Burns was nowhere to be found, but I heard him everywhere. In all the busy city streets he spoke to me clearly, over and over, but I could not find him anywhere. There was only his muttering voice, constant and in my ears.

Rebecca was standing beside the counter in the record store. "He's not here," she said when I asked. "I don't know where he is." She was leaning on the counter wearing tight jeans and an ivory sweater the color of old piano keys. It left her midriff bare and let the little button of her navel peak out when she moved. She was round in all the round places, firm in all the firm places. It was obvious why Mick Burns wanted into those jeans. "Are you all right, J. B.?" she said.

As I told her about the missing bottle of wine, she was staring at a guy with carved biceps who strolled into the store. He stared back at her. But neither of them smiled. It was way too serious for that. "Yeah, he was really pissed," she said. "We went up there, and he was telling me the whole way like about how great this wine was supposed to be. Then he like opened the refrigerator and acted like he couldn't find it. So he got like really pissed off."

"Did he blame me?" I said.

"You mean there really was a bottle of wine?" Her voice was nasal and it squeaked around the end of each sentence, but you could overlook it when you stood next to those jeans, with the little button navel squeezing out of that soft white tummy. "I thought it was like just a line," she whined through her nose as her eyes followed the biceps across the front of the store. "You know, Mick," she said, "he's always got a line. Now he says he's gonna like make a record." She laughed at that. It was a cackle designed to wheedle under your nerves, as if some low grade fever hiding an infection was due to endanger your whole system. But there was still that roundness to her ivory sweater.

"You don't know where he is now?" I asked. I didn't tell her that Mick Burns' record deal was no more of a line than that bottle of wine.

She shrugged her ivory sweater and I knew she would be no more help. But I had to find Mick, I had to explain to him what had happened. Even if I missed this record date, even if I was too late and the roster was set or something, he needed to know it wasn't me. Because there would be more dates, club shows instead of working the streets. There would be a tour to sell the record, you know, there would be interviews and articles and reviews now. I needed to be part of that ride. It was dream come true time, and I needed to talk to Mick.

I walked down the street, resisting the urge to run, looking for him. My body wanted to run, to find him now. I went by his apartment, I walked through the corner grocery along the way, to the bakery and the butcher shop near his place. I stopped at a couple of corner taverns, at the pool hall down two blocks from his place. I walked around to the street corner were we played. But he was nowhere to be found. He was gone.

I couldn't find him anywhere, but I could hear him whispering, "You can't cut it, J. B." in my ears. Except now I knew it was wrong. I knew it was only the wine. It was Hemp that had screwed up, and not me. And he wouldn't be mad at Hemp. He couldn't be.

And when he saw the mistake he'd made, I would be back in. In the band. In the session. In the music. And in the silence that came with it.

Then the whispering in my ears could stop. "You can't cut it, Jan."

The oily grime on my hands swirls down the drain with the water and the soap, leaving the porcelain white as the bar of soap my hands hold. I look at myself in the mirror and I see my own eyes gazing back at me from out of all the dirty, matted hair. With one of my hands I pull the paper hat off and drop it on the floor. My eyes look back into my eyes from the mirror. There is a light inside there. I lean over and cup the clean water in my hands, and I wash it into my face and deep into the wrinkles and pockets around my eyes. The water is cool, so clear, so simple. I hear the rush of the faucet, I hear the gurgling of the drain. And over it I hear, in the distance, his clarinet singing and singing the blues.

And that is all I hear.

I walked up to a wine sellers window on Lexington, and the dark green bottles were lying on their sides in the racks inside. It stopped me right there. I couldn't find Mick anywhere. He had disappeared. But his voice kept echoing around in my mind.

I put my palms up against the window glass, and gazed in at all those bottles and suddenly it became clear to me. The sun on the glass was in my hands, and in the reflection I saw a policeman strolling toward me. He was watching me carefully and he said, "Jan, are you okay?" And I said to his reflection in the glass, "I can't cut it." He quickened his step and said, "Son, air yoo ill right?" But it was hard to hear him, because of all the whispering around me, all the voices in the street saying over and over, "I'm going to be making some changes, Jan. I'm gonna be making some changes, Jan." In the reflection of the window I could see the outline of my body, hands up and pressed against the glass. But I couldn't see my face. My face is just a blank, a dark, empty smear filled with whatever stood beyond it: bottles and barrels and cymbals and snares.

And then I know it isn't the wine, it isn't some bottle missing, some night inside her jeans that didn't work out. It wasn't getting into anybody's jeans. I know it is just a trying to keep all the voices quiet. I know I am just fooling myself, because this has nothing to do with wine, or Rebecca's sweet jeans, or Hemp's thirsty soul. Now it is all me. Just me alone. And nothing else.

A loud snap crinkles across the sky, and the window I hold in my hands shatters into a thousand shards of light. The sun and the sky disappear in my hands, and the cop who is yelling at me now, I can hear him mixed with all the others yelling at me, but he has disappeared too, he's gone in the sparkle and the crash.

And now it is not just my face that is a blank smear, filled with the empty, raw material of the world. I am gone too. My face, my shoulders, my chest, my hands thrust up in the air, they all have vanished into the shattering light.

The cop, somewhere behind me, is yelling, "Hey! Hey!" And it is all me, and it is all yelling at me. The cop puts his hand on my shoulder and turns me around. Glass falls from my shoulders and my hair, it crunches under my feet, and sirens and alarms are screaming in the air, screaming, "Cut it, cut it, cut it!" Over and over.

The cop looks at me, with worry and concern all over his face, and he says something, but it makes no sense. He mutters noise, and nonsense leaks at me from out of his mouth, and I can't hear him. He takes hold of my arm at the elbow. His grip is firm and tight. He is talking to me all the time, but it is just noise. I say, "Leave me alone." His face draws back away from me at that, but his grip tightens. "Leave me alone," I say again, and I see fear in his face now. But he is not afraid of me, I know that because he's a cop. He is afraid of what he doesn't understand, of what he doesn't understand in me. And it is there that I have him. Because I know now that I don't understand at all.

He tries to lead me down the street and take me away. But I know I can't let him do that. He doesn't understand me. He'll try to hide what he doesn't understand. With a quick pull, I jerk my arm free of his grip. He's startled, because I seem so helpless and confused to him. But I know he is the one who is confused. I turn and I run straight away. He yells more noise at me, and then runs after me, for a few steps, and then he yells some more, but I crash through the sidewalks and run across the middle of the street, and make the horns blare and the brakes screech and the cabbies scream at me in a dozen languages I hear but I don't understand, and I leave that cop in my dust. I fly, fly away through it all. And worst of all, the noise of the sirens and the horns and the yells quiets the roaring whispers in my ears. The more the cop and all of his kind yell at me, the less I hear. The less I can hear from all that matters. In my noise hides my quiet, and the peace it bears.

"God bless the child," I always sing as I sweep the Mail Box floor at night, "God bless the child who's got his own."

In the morning I will have to wash the windows. You just can't believe how smudged and dirty the big glass double door to the Mail Box gets in just one day. All those fingerprints. People just can't use the steel handles, you know. They've got to put their hands right on the glass. It is as if the clarity of it tempts them.

"Papa may have," I sing, as I sweep the dust away.

But I don't mind, really. Wiping the glass clear every morning when I come in to work gives me a satisfaction I really can't explain. It is beyond understanding. The windows and doors come so clean so easily, and so well. It is so clear and sparkling every morning when we unlock the doors.

Bernie likes it this way, too. It makes her happy to have the doors so clean, so the customers are happy. And the regional managers of the Mail Box, when they come in they don't notice the doors, because they're clear as the glass they are made from, and that makes Bernie happy. "Looks good, Johnny," she says and smiles, thinking of how good she will look when UPS arrives.

But at night, like tonight, when Bernie and everyone else is gone, and all the customers have gone and only their boxes remain, waiting to be shipped away into the morning, and I'm alone in the quiet, I sweep the floor. It is my favorite part of the day. Of every day.

"Mama may have," I sing as I push the big broom around.

It's the bar-oosh, bar-oosh rhythm of the big broom that I love. It is still so comforting to hear it beat out the measures, to feel the pulse of the melody, to let it swing through the end of the day. It takes me back to Chico playing for the Lady, I remember standing backstage and the way she squeezed my hand.

"But God bless the child," I sing to the regular swish, swish of the broom, like brushes on a snare.

And sometimes, when it is dark and cold and winter in the back room and the morning seems far away, I hear him play the clarinet, the way he let it sing at Carnegie Hall on the night when the music took me back, when his tone pulled me in the big green door and washed my face in the mirror of his chalumeau, and took me up from the streets and lifted me until I could hear again. His clarinet sang until I could hear the silence again, all around me. The quiet of everyday.

But that's when I let it stop. I never go past that point anymore, past the place where the broom strikes the floor in a comfortable swing, and I hum along with the tune, and sometimes at night at the Mail Box I break out and sing. "God bless the child," I sing.

But never go farther. Don't slip past that simple beat. I speak now for you, for all of us. Hold it there. Go no further. Not a measure more, because, because. That way perdition lies, I tell you, and the whispering street always waits. It lies in wait like a hungry cat, hissing in the dark. Patient, but always there. Waiting to pounce. Unless I know enough to turn way.

"God bless the child," I sing, "who's got his own." And I remember that trembling deep within the hungry grip of the Lady's hand. I squeeze my hands tight around handle of the broom, around her, and I hold it all still.

Private Bouts

"He's gonnna git himself beat down."

"Who is?"

"This Willard Boy. The 'Potawatamie Giant.' Jack's gone beat him down."

"What are you talking about?"

Ike leaned up against the door. It was cracked to let in some light, and Robert was sitting where he could look out and see the countryside. Robert knew just before they hit Gainesville, they'd be in Texas. He wanted to see it, when they crossed the line.

"It says here this white kid—this Jess Willard—he's gone git to scrap with Jack Johnson." Ike laughed. He was holding a page out of some newspaper, a torn piece of the days old sports news. "They gone fight down in Havana, at a race track." Ike snorted, cleared his throat, spit at the floor. "Old Jack don't fight here no more. It's not safe here. It's not even safe for him to live here no more." Ike was running his finger along the line of print then. A corner of the torn page flapped in the wind that came through the cracked door.

It made Robert think how long it had been since he'd seen a newspaper, since before all this furor with Texas anyway. He used to read the papers often. But lately the only big news was some British ship sunk by the Germans, or another fruitless battle in France or Greece or Turkey. It all sounded the same to him, so there wasn't much to miss in the papers these days.

"He gone git his pale little behind beat," Ike scoffed.

"But that Jess Willard's a pretty tough kid, isn't he?" Robert said. The tone in Ike's voice was mean. It made Robert feel like standing up for this young fighter Willard. "That's what I've heard anyway. He's called the Potawatamie Giant. Right?"

"Sure, but nobody's good as Jack, cause Jack be the Galveston Giant," Ike shook his head proudly. "Jack Johnson's got a right fist that big, Robert." The old man put his two fists together, one on top of the other, and shook them in the air. "I know Jack," Ike said, throwing his head back. "I met him once. He had a niggruh trainer used to buy booze from Pappy June, when they came through Chicago. Back when Jack was just starting up, trying to git in the ring with white fighters. Jack came down with his trainer one day, and he went around and shook everybody's hand." Ike waved his two fists in the air, like he was getting ready to swing. Slowly, they dropped to his side again. "When Jack made it to the top, they never came through Chicago anymore. I guess they could buy their liquor store-made then." Then he chuckled at some memory he didn't want to share. He said, "That man be some nigger, Mister Mahon. Believe me, his left fist's the size of a sledge hammer. Jess Willard let his chin connect with them knuckles just once, and he be peeling his little white pants off the canvas for a long, long time to come."

"Well, we'll see, won't we?" Robert laughed. Ike went back to reading the paper again, his finger on the page. The train was slowing down for another stop, the whistle blowing, and a sign flashed by the crack.

Crusher Springs, Okla.

pop. 17

Someone had scrawled under that in chalk at the bottom of the sign: "At Home." It was just another stop, but still they weren't in Texas.

"It's gone be one of them no-limit fights," Ike said, still gazing at the paper. "They fight till one of them drops." He was quiet a moment, scanning up and down the page. Then he sighed. "I do pity that poor Willard boy," he said, and seemed suddenly to mean it.

"Johnson's getting pretty old for that, isn't he, Ike? A fight like that could go thirty rounds."

Ike Waters slapped a hand to his cheek. He let his mouth hang wide open, showing the gaps in his teeth. He looked like some old grandmother who just bet on the winning horse at a country fair.

"Oh Lord, Robert Mahon. Don't you know? Age don't git a man," he said, holding in his baritone laugh. "It's in the spirit. That's what gits a man. You're not old till you give up fighting, son. Don't you know that?" Then he let loose and laughed out loud, and the gray whiskers on his chin quivered.

"Jess Willard is going to git his behind beat," he said. "He is in some kind of big trouble now. Big trouble, son," he shook his head sadly. "Some kind of trouble, I say."

The Texas Rover crossed the Red River at sunset. Sitting across from Ike in the baggage car, Robert saw the water, shining red as its name in the sunlight, and he knew they were in Texas. In a few minutes, the train stopped for quarter of an hour at Gainesville. Normally he wouldn't get out for so short a stop, like this Gainesville stop, but it was different this time. They were in Texas, by God, Texas.

He jumped down and ran up alongside the Rover until he saw her in the window. There was no platform at the Gainesville station, so the window was high above his head, more than an arm's reach. He could see her staring through the glass, but she looked over his head at the station, and she didn't see him. So he jumped up and rapped on the pane, with a grin the size of a Texas tale on his face.

All he did was startle her. Lucy jumped in her seat, and she looked down at him curtly. He just waved both his hands in the air, telling her to open the window. They didn't have time for being prissy or mad. Not now.

When she finally pulled it up, the window screeched like it hadn't been opened in months.

"We're in Texas, honey. We made it."

"Fort Worth?" she stuck her head out of the car, and then her shoulders. There was still no smile on her face.

"No, Gainesville," he cried over a rushing steam vent on the engine up ahead. "Where's the boys?"

"They're over there with Jason yet."

"Who?"

"What are we going to do in Fort Worth?"

"About what?"

She didn't answer for a moment. "About that man. That old man you picked up in Kansas City."

"Ike?" Robert said. "We'll buy him another ticket."

He thought about the money, and he wondered then if Ike would care to be bumming a ride again. It'd sure be fine with Robert if he did. When the crippled, old man was caught by a rail dick in Kansas City, Robert felt sorry for him, and bought him a ticket to Fort Worth, to keep him out of jail. It was after that Ike offered to come along to Texas as a "hired hand." Robert still liked the idea of having a man to help him get started out there. Even if he was just an old club-footed colored.

"How much will that cost?"

"I don't know. Not much."

She said nothing.

"How you like Texas?" He laughed and threw an arm up like he was presenting her to some dandy. Then he turned, as if to look the dandy over himself. "Don't look like nothing special. Does it."

She was still hanging out the window, and not speaking. She looked out at the landscape, a flatiron of green grass turning yellow in the new sunset. "No, it doesn't look like anything special," she said.

He had married Lucy five years ago, but she still seemed like a stranger sometimes. For those five years they struggled to get by on rented land, and about the only thing they had to show for it now were the two boys, Jack and Vince. They could have raised those kids in town, and have more to show for it.

But Robert wanted his sons reared in the country, where'd they know what a good day's work was, and where their old man could leave something behind for them, something more than paper and schooling. Something made of dirt.

"Hey, did you hear how the Texan busted his ass raking leaves?" Robert yelled up to her as the train huffed again.

She was looking at the yellow sand around the tracks now.

"He had to ride bareback to Missouri to find some," Robert Mahon laughed at his own joke.

"He scares me, Robert. I don't like him."

"Who?" Robert heard a conductor calling, "All 'board."

"That man you found. That colored man."

Robert kicked at the dry sand beside the train. The whistle blew a long blast. He thought of how nice it must be on those cushioned seats in the car. But there was money too be saved when he rode with the freight. Money they were going to need to get started on the two hundred acres of grass that he'd bought in the Valparaiso.

"Oh now, you just don't know Ike. Give him a chance, Lucy, would you?"

"You are, aren't you?" When she looked down at him, her eyes were black and angry. "You're gonna haul him all the way down here too. Aren't you."

The train whistle blew twice. She looked out at the bank of clouds cutting up into the scarlet sun in the west. "What if he dies on us?" she said. "What if he's just tagging along waiting to die?"

"What in . . ." The engine blew a few, long shots of steam, bellying up for a run. "What are you talking about, Lucy?" he said.

She let her shoulders ease back into the coach. Only her head was sticking out the window. The whistle blew again, one long blast.

"Don't you care about us?" she said to him. "Don't you give a damn about me? Am I just the last thing you put on the train?"

"Lucy. Hey, Lucy, don't talk like that." The train beat one pull into the wheels. "What's the matter with you?" The whistle still blew, and through its squall the engine pulled another beat.

"I got to get back to the freighter, Lucy." He had to take a couple of steps, keeping pace with the train. She just watched him out the window.

"I'm all right," she said to him, and he saw her standing up to close the window. "I love you," she said without anything in her eyes. "Don't worry about me," and then the window closed, with a distant thud.

Robert ran alongside the car for a dozen steps or so, but she wouldn't look back at him. The train kept gaining speed. It was building steam while Robert lost his wind. The dull red cars creaked and swayed past him, the strangers' faces looked down at him from the windows. He thought, 'Oh shit, now I'm going to miss it.'

"Git your hands out," he heard Ike call to him. His feet pounded wearily in the sand and he sensed people in the Gainesville station watching him.

Ike stood in the wide open doorway of the freighter. He had wrapped one arm around a steel handle, and he held the other out for Robert. As Robert grabbed the old man's hand and ran alongside the car, Ike slowly pulled him out of his stride, and with a leap Robert was sitting on the freight car floor.

Then the old man laughed at him. "You'll never make a no good bum hopping rails that way. There won't always be old Ike to help you out. And Mister Mahon, I must say, you run like a pregnant mammy." Ike leaned his crooked back against the door. The twist in the poor man's back was nearly as bad as the one in his foot.

"Shit," was all Robert said, panting. After he caught his breath, he muttered, "Damn it all."

Ike left him alone. The old man watched from under his gray brows, wrinkling up his nose a couple of times like an animal being wary, and he let Robert sulk. Robert kept his eyes on the cinders that sped by in a blur outside.

It was dark by the time the train left Sanger, Texas. South of Peterson's Spur somewhere it clouded over so the stars were gone. A mist was settling in when they stopped in Blue Mound, and now, outside Fort Worth, they were digging through a full, dense fog.

Robert Mahon sat silent for most of the way, until finally Ike said, "Friend, it ain't doing you no good cooking there alone."

So Robert cussed her out then. "Damned woman, she wouldn't know a goddamned son of a bitchin' chance if she saw it sitting next to her." He went on with more but after a while Ike Waters stopped him with his silence.

"You don't mean no word a that," Waters told him.

Robert didn't care to hear that from anyone, especially someone he'd known only a day or two. He didn't think the way he felt could be so obvious.

"She's hurting you something fierce," Ike said. "So say what you mean, Mister Mahon, sir."

But instead Robert shut up, and he sat on they bench seat, feeling all put upon and sorry for himself. He certainly didn't deserve to be treated like this. The train stopped at nearly a dozen little towns, while he just sat and scowled, so Ike Waters ignored him. The old man found a comfortable carpet bag, stuffed with soft clothes, laid his head on it and promptly fell asleep. When they pulled into Fort Worth, Robert stood up quietly and hopped out of the freighter. Ike never stirred until after Robert was gone.

The fog outside was thick and black with the night, but Robert could still make out the station lights. He walked alongside the train until he found Lucy's car. Inside there were small electric lights running along each wall of the coach.

She was gone, but Jack and Vince were there. Jack was squirming around in the seat next to Joey Delahanty, the man Robert had met at some little station back in Kansas, the big bellied man who said he was going to the Valparaiso to farm too. Delahanty's skinny wife was trying to put the kids to bed. Vince was nearly asleep on her lap, but Jack was giving her a hard time, poking at his little brother's leg from across Delahanty's fat belly. Little Vince would squeal at that, and Delahanty would laugh. They stopped when Robert walked up. He told Jack to settle down and behave, but they were just holding still until Father was gone, and everyone present knew that, too. Everyone but the two boys who probably would only find out when they started to squirm around again. When Robert asked, Delahanty looked surprised and said Lucy was outside, out for a walk or something. "I thought she was gone looking for you," the fat man said.

Robert headed for the lights in the station then. There were a lot of people wandering around in the fog, so he had to be careful. It was so thick he could easily walk right into someone. He found the main door to the depot, but she wasn't there. In the light of the station, inside, everything was clear and crisp. He looked through a window and saw a middle-aged woman. She stood by the ticket booth, where there was a stalky, flowerless geranium on the counter, and she was reading a schedule. Her hands in the clear light were so white he saw a tinge of blue veins in them. Her blonde hair was going gray slightly, but her face and her hands looked worn and old. She was the only woman inside the depot.

Robert waited a few minutes walking back and forth in front of the doorway, glancing in now and then, and looking at that woman. Finally he stuck his face against the window glass, but he knew she wasn't in there, and he knew she wasn't trying to find him, or she would be meeting him at the station door.

Maybe she was back on the coach, he thought. They had missed each other somehow in the fog. So he ran his fingers through his dirty hair, trying at least to straighten it, and he walked back toward the tracks. On his way to the train, wandering in the mist, he found her. She was leaning against a wooden pillar, alone, staring at the fog like it was a beast waiting for her out there.

She looked over at him, but her face showed no recognition. He could think of nothing to say.

So he put a hand on her cheek. Her face was hot, and the heat surprised him. When they had stood like that for a moment, it started to rain. Big, scattered drops fell, the kind of rain that would cut the fog by morning, if it kept up.

"How much farther do we have left?" she said.

"Not far now," he put his hand around the back of her neck. Then he pulled her close to him, held her and touched her hair with his hand. His fingers traced the bottom of the tight knot she wore in her hair. "We're almost there now," he said, and tried to make it sound comforting and sure. "We'll be all right," he said, softly. They folded together like a pair of hands, and he felt the warmth hidden in her. She didn't say word, because she was still distracted.

They walked along the tracks, not talking much, just a word or two here and there as she held onto him. Robert kept his hand in her hair, and he loosened it until it fell free.

"Why are we coming here?" she said.

He thought about how to answer her, but he didn't speak. She just couldn't seem to understand the chance he was taking. He only wanted to be somebody for a change, to own the land he lived on, be his own free man. The frontier he'd heard about since he was a kid, it was closing up. There wasn't much left. This one shot might be the last chance he had. But that didn't seem to matter to her.

When they had wandered somewhere past the train, where the shape of the caboose was barely visible, he heard Ike calling out to him through the fog.

"Robert, is that you?" Ike yelled, coming toward them. Out of the fog, following Ike Waters along the tracks, a black man appeared. In the mist around him, the stranger's feet did not seem to touch the ground.

"Over here," Robert yelled.

"You got to hear this, Robert." Ike smiled, and nodded politely to the woman. "You've got to hear it too, ma'am," he said.

The stranger moved up alongside Ike. He was wearing some sort of train uniform that fit him just a little tight. He was short, a potbelly sagged in his shirt, and on top of his low head, the man tucked his white hair inside a jockey's cap: a blue and shining orange jockey's cap, tilted off to one side. He sported a thin goatee as white as the fog around the lights.

"This be the Switch Man," Ike said. "Tell them what you seen, Switch Man."

"You all are the folks going down to the Valparaiso Valley?" The Switch Man asked. "Is that where you're going, sir?"

Robert nodded; he looked down at the black man's hands hanging limply near his baggy pockets, and at the pockets bulging with God only knew what, pockets bulging full of secrets.

The Switch Man chuckled, "And you are going along, too, Isaac?"

"Tell them what you seen, would you?" Ike said.

"Oh and this young lady, too. Well, what dare I say?"

The Switch Man wrinkled up his eyes, and a toothy grin split his lips. He nodded his head yes, to himself.

He was an important man, Robert thought as he waited for him to speak. He was important, the switchman of the yard. In his hands he held the lives of passengers and coachmen, depot masters and engineers, conductors and even the people on the platform waving their farewells. When the Switch Man did his job right, and he had to do it right, the trains passed through the depot safely and easily. They hummed past one another, rattling in opposite directions, maybe reaching thirty miles an hour, sometimes just inches apart, and all in the Switch Man's hands.

"The Valparaiso, sir, is like nothing you have ever seen," his head kept nodding. "But you listen to me. There's a fortune to be made down there. There's a fortune lying beneath that grass," Robert felt Lucy's grip tighten around his waist. 'By God,' he thought, 'maybe now she knows what I'm trying to do.'

"Lord, Lord, Robert, the Switch Man, he's been there," Ike shouted it out, and he whistled through a gap in his teeth. Then he jumped in the air, or he danced, Robert wasn't sure which. But Ike swung his twisted foot in the air, and shuffled with his good foot on the ground.

"But you listen to me now," the Switch Man said, "listen good. There is a fortune waiting. But it's not for just everybody. You better be tough. Don't let anybody mess with you, or rile you up, and you better be tough down there." He beat a hand above his pot belly, and the second time his hand struck hollowly on his chest. "But if you are tough, deep down in your intestinal soul, you'll find your fortune. If it is in you to do that, you'll find it."

"Are there many folks down there?" Robert asked.

"Oh. There's a sufficiency, sir." His mouth curled up under his straggly mustache, and the lips disappeared. He became silent, as if he'd said all he was going to say.

Lucy's arm slipped away from Robert's waist. "Are they grazing with it mostly?" Robert said, "Or what is it? Is it fenced yet?" She kissed him on the cheek, near his ear.

"No. No." The Switch Man said, "Not many fences. Not there. "

"I'm going back to see how the kids are doing;" she whispered to him. Robert squeezed her shoulder where he still held her, and nodded. "Sure, honey," he whispered. But there were things he had to know now.

As she walked away back toward the train, he was asking the Switch Man, "What kind of cattle are they grazing?" The old man chortled, and he seemed to be playing the fool now.

"Just talk up, will you?" Ike was perturbed. "Say what you seen," he said, "Switch Man."

*

The rain had stopped slowly. It was only a cloud passing over the fog. She walked along keeping the cars in sight. The caboose with its pale electric lanterns was the hardest car to find, because it was the first part of the train she came to through the fog. Then she walked in the gravel and cinders beside two freight cars. Another freighter sat up ahead in the thick mist. With every step its hard lines grew clearer; the timber struts lining its sides grew into blacker shadows. She wondered if she was walking beside the wrong train.

"Hey, where are you headed in such a rush?" It was Jason's voice, but she couldn't see him. She stopped and looked around.

"Where are you?" she muttered.

"Right here," he said, matter of factly. Then he emerged like a piece of the night from the dark beside the train. At first he was just a shadow, but slowly she made out the details of his body. His hands were stuffed in his pants pockets. He smiled crookedly. And his eyes were still hidden in the shadow of his brow.

"Headed back to the coach?" he said. Jason Henry eased up beside her. She noticed his shirt collar was open. He was not wearing his tie. "May I escort this lovely lady to her seat?" He spoke jokingly, but that didn't hide the insistence in his voice. His smile turned a little, twisting straighter on his face.

"Of course," she said. She had met him after the train left Kansas City. Robert had taken the two boys for a while, riding with him in the baggage car, so she was alone when Jason Henry sat down across from her.

He was a rail service inspector. It seemed he'd been almost everywhere, and he told her stories about everyplace he'd seen. She urged him on. Any place seemed better than where she was going. Just last night, when she couldn't sleep in her seat, Jason Henry sat across from her and told her about Atlanta, Georgia, and Santa Fe and San Francisco. He told her that in just a few nights he would be sitting at the bar inside Mame's on Bourbon Street, and there'd be music playing so sweet and sad it made you shake your head and want to sing. How nice it was to hear Jason Henry's voice, when she could slouch down in her seat and feel along the pretty lace trim on her dress with the tips of her fingers, feel how delicate it was. His voice was clean and full of afternoon sun, while it spun out naughty Arabian night tales of dark singers and deep blue love, just the way she once imagined it could be. The kind of stories no one thought to tell a Texas farmer's wife.

So now he took her hand and he wrapped it through the crook of his arm. And he led her through the fog, he pressed her arm tightly against his ribs. She could feel his chest rise and fall with his every breath.

"Some night, huh?" he said.

"Sometimes I like the fog though," she said. They were alongside another boxcar then, and he was walking very slowly. Her skirt brushed against his leg as they stepped. "Everything looks different in a fog," she kept talking, "if you can see at all."

He stopped there and hung onto her arm. They were beside a gritty freight car, so close she could smell the grime, padded with dust, on its walls. Or maybe it was the dirty fog she smelled. Without letting go of her arm, he reached across and touched her hair with his other hand. "I like your hair down, Lucy." He looked straight in her eyes and slid his hand down to her neck. His fingertips were soft on her skin.

"When we get to Temple, I'll be switching trains," he said. "I'll be in Austin for a day, and them I'm headed for New Orleans. By the end of the week." He ran his thumb delicately along her cheek with his fingers still touching her neck. His smile slowly disappeared.

He waited for her to speak then. But Lucy had nothing to say. She heard the grunt of some animal in the freighter behind her. Then Jason Henry leaned toward her and his thigh and shoulder touched her, and stayed there, gently touching her.

"Come with me," he said flatly, and Lucy wished he had at least whispered it. "We'll be in New Orleans on Sunday, Lucy."

She wasn't the slightest bit surprised. It was as if she had been waiting for the idea to come, hoping for his proposal, any kind of chance, to go away. But now that it had happened, it did not seem so strange, or even so important.

She started to speak. But he put a finger on her lips. Then his finger slipped away and drew an outline on her eyebrows. He was staring at her hair, as if she had no face.

She took his hand in hers and tapped it with her fingertips. "Jason Henry," she said like a school marm, "Behave yourself." She grinned at him teasingly.

As if he hadn't heard, he slid a hand behind her neck and his head bent down to her shoulder. He kissed her at the base of the neck. She whispered something, trying to stop him—she would never remember what it was she said—he but his arm just slipped out of hers and wrapped around her waist. Then she could feel him breathe around her collar. With her free hand she reached around and grabbed his coat, and she put her hand on his chest and pushed at him expecting him to back away at her slightest touch. He kissed her neck again and muttered something.

Before she realized what was happening, with this face pressed close behind hers, he forced her up against a wall of the railway car. Then he pushed his body against her. His weight forced her off balance. She felt a steel strut on the car pressed against her spine, and the edge of the freighter's floor jutted across her lower back. Everywhere she smelled the grime of the boxcar. And then Lucy did not know if she could even breathe. She heard, as if it came from someone else, the sound of her own voice, and she said his name through her teeth.

Instinctively, out of fear and not thought, she twisted a shoulder against his chest and tried to free herself. But he picked her up and slammed her against the freighter, and his whole weight pressed her against it. Her feet were dangling back against the wheels. "I won't hurt you," he said, and she felt the lump of his sex pressed on her thigh.

Jason Henry pushed her down between the cars. When she struggled again, feeling the world like a trap door slamming closed, he shoved her across the gravel that lay around the tracks. Her leg struck the steel edge of a wheel. Lucy felt a sharp pain there, and at the same moment all of her emotions seemed to flow away. She was empty, like a bucket kicked over. He knelt down around her legs, pinning her to the ground, and suddenly, unaccountably, she felt no fear.

Then he rose up on his knees and uncovered his erect penis. He touched himself, and his hands trembled. He stared at her legs and knelt there holding himself. She heard his breath quaver as he inhaled. Then, welling up out of the emptiness inside her, she laughed. She could not keep it in, anymore than she could say what she laughed at. But one burst of laughter came from deep in her, like the tap of a stranger's finger on her shoulder from above, or from below, and then it was gone.

He glanced at her face, and looked away quickly. But when he leaned forward, reaching out to touch her sex through the cotton cloth, he freed one of her legs.

Almost without knowing why, she jerked her knee up into him, she kicked his pelvic bone hard with her shin. Though she couldn't feel it, she knew her knee must have landed square on him.

He groaned wetly, and he curled back around his stomach. So Lucy pulled her legs free. She rolled over once or twice feeling like a hollow drum, and then she crawled out from under the freight car. Not knowing where to go, she turned and ran, searching for the passenger cars hidden in the fog.

Strange, empty rail cars developed out of the mist. Their details, the hard rails and the wooden slatting, the lines of the A.T. and the numbers on their doors, appeared just seconds before she left them behind in the dank night, and they melted away into the fog. But she did not feel herself running. She was floating, flying along in the air. She had no contact with the cinders and dirt on the ground.

A low baggage cart jumped out of the mist in front of her. She didn't even think to turn, because she believed she would glide right over it, but it caught her ankle with its flat edge, and she tripped and fell on her knees in loose gravel. She put her hands on the ground, amazed that she could even touch it. The rocks pressed her palms, she stood up and began to walk.   The night air was wet and close, and now she breathed hard in it. The scraped skin on her knees ached, but she walked quickly, and she watched that nothing came at her from out of the fog.   She turned away from the train then, realizing that was where Jason Henry would look for her, and she felt her feet in the cinders.

A wooden pillar of the station entrance developed out of the mist. Lucy walked past it and away from the lights of the station house.   She found an empty set of tracks in the dark, and walked beside them, unconsciously leaving herself a trail to find her way home. Behind her she could see a glow in the fog that was the station yard, halos of lanterns lit here and there, and an engine somewhere rasped with steam. The world back there seemed an angry animal.

As she wandered in the dark, Lucy stumbled onto a three-foot post with a red glass and the number six at its base. At its peak, a bracket for holding a lantern was empty. There was the lever to a switch slanting off in the dark beside it. So Lucy sat down and rested her back against the wooden post. She slid her feet back and forth, pushing cinders aside, until she felt smooth sand under her shoes. Sand would run deep, and it was soft.

Then it occurred to her that no one would be looking for her. She was, in an odd way, free. The boys were with Delahanty, and they might even be asleep. Robert figured she was back on the train, tucking Jack and Vince away for the night. And Jason Henry, he would be afraid to look for her now. He'd be afraid she had found Robert, or someone.

She closed her eyes and leaned her head back on the post. She was tender where he had hurled her against the boxcar. A dog was barking in the dark. Its yap mixed with the indiscriminate yells and hollers of men in the rail yard. There was the metallic clank and grind of steel wheels on the rails, interrupted by the whine of brakes.

Through it all, just like a figure growing out of the fog, Lucy began to hear crickets. She sat and listened, concentrating on the sound of the insects in the dark, until slowly the chirping was louder than the noise of the men in the train yard, until all she heard was their simple chirp.

Suddenly, right beside her, the metal switch screeched. She looked up and saw that old colored man in his bright satin cap pushing with all his weight against the switch. He seemed to have come from nowhere. The metal screeched again, and the switch locked in place.

"Excuse me, ma'am," he said, "I didn't mean to disturb you. You looked mighty comfortable there." His eyes seemed to shine clearly through the wrinkled dark around them. They seemed almost lit from behind. "I like that spot myself." He chuckled, "It's not as nice as number nine though. You ought to try that one. Number nine. That one is nice and soft, yes, ma'am."

Lucy glanced down and saw the dirt and a small tear on her skirt about her knees. She almost couldn't say where it had come from.

"Say," the old man said, "aren't you the lady who's . . ."

She nodded her head.

"Well, my woman! This is no time for a rest." He shook a crooked finger at her, and the white line of it was ghostly in the dark. "You better get yourself going or you'll miss your ride down to the Valparaiso. Get up, woman. Git yourself going now," he clucked.

When she moved her legs to rise, the old man muttered, "I got to git on by number five before the midnight freight comes through." Lucy realized, after a moment, he was talking to himself. He turned and walked away following the tracks, as if she wasn't there. Lucy stood up and touched the grease in her hair at the back of her head. The old man was nothing but a shadow in the mist when he turned around again and said, "You take care of my friend Isaac, now, little lady. He's had it rough." And the old railroad man backed away into the dark. After he was gone, she could still hear him mumbling to himself, the sound of his voice mixed with the wet chirp of the crickets and the crisp clank of steel, until slowly the crickets seemed to speak with his voice. "Git you. Goin' now," the crickets said. "Git you. Goin' now. Woman."

The train whistle blew twice again, and she knew the train would depart soon, on some other track, and that from this switch she couldn't see it, she'd just hear the wheels rattle and the steam roar somewhere in the dark. She knew the lights would be on in the coach where Jack and Vince were sleeping. The coach would be only half full with sleepy night riders. There would be empty seats again, just like there were last night. The faces in the car would all be familiar; not the same, but they would all look the same. Lucy thought about sitting down again, leaning against the post and listening for the Rover to run by. She wanted to sit down there and rest her head on her curled knees and go to sleep. Now she could fall away to sleep and sleep away the night.

But she knew something was different in her, something that was more than just an emotion. Something further down. She heard that verse her mother had always quoted, the one that seemed so lost and sad, that went: "You got to lose a thing before you can find it." That was so simple, but it was not easy, or even sensible. It just seemed honest; it sounded in her thoughts like the dark inside of her mother's cedar trunk.

So Lucy started to walk back toward the warm glow of the station, though if someone stopped her and asked her why, she couldn't say. Slowly the murmur of voices grew louder, and then the lights were clearer. "Get that in there," she heard a yell. And distantly, "This God forsaken fog." When she got within the lights of the train, she heard the conductor's voice, the same man's voice she'd heard at every stop since Kansas City, only a little hoarser now, and a little older. "Board for Crowley, Keeler, Joshua, Weatherford Junction. For Bosco, Crawford, Waco, and Temple," it croaked. Temple, she thought, was where the road split; Temple was where one fork led to New Orleans and the other to a Texas farm. And New Orleans was nothing more than the gritty underside of a boxcar now.

Lucy walked alongside the Texas Rover without hurrying. The engine blasted a long roar at the whistle. She found her coach and stepped onto the stairwell. The minute her feet hit the metal of that stairway they began to hurt, and in the dim lights she saw the sand and grease on her skirt. The tear along her knee was bigger than she'd thought. But at that moment she didn't care.

Inside the coach Joey Delahanty stood up and came toward her. "Lucy. There you are. We thought you'd missed the train. But Mr. Henry said he saw you with your husband. He said he saw you back at the freight car, with Robert." Delahanty smiled good naturedly.

"Where is he?"

"Pardon?" Delahanty leaned toward her. "I couldn't hear you."

"Where is Jason Henry?"

"Oh," Delahanty scratched behind his ear, "he took his things." The fat man said, "It was kind of odd. He said he had to go, he had another seat. Or something like that. All in a big hurry."

"I just knew you wouldn't leave those boys alone," Alvina Delahanty said to her.

Lucy looked down the aisle to her seat, while Delahanty said, "Oh don't you worry, Vinnie took good care of them. Like they were her own." She saw the two boys lying in the sleeper. But she could hardly believe that they were asleep, and that this world inside the coach was still in order. How could those children dare to be in asleep? How could the world act so orderly?

"They've been sleeping since you left."

"Those are some good boys you got there, Mrs. Mahon. Full of spunk." Delahanty laughed. "Why just . . . "

"I think the train ride is catching up with them," Lucy said. Something told her there was no point in saying what had happened. How could they even know what was out in that fog? There was no way to know, unless you wandered out there.

"You look like you could use some rest yourself," Delahanty put a hand on her shoulder, and his lips broke into a kindly grin.

Alvina said, "You get some sleep, dear." She clasped her hands in front of her, and she said, "We'll keep an eye on those two boys."

Lucy walked away without saying another word, turning her back to them. The train was reaching full speed by the time she finally sat down. She stared along the steel rail, that formed the rim of the sleeper, and at the edge of her vision she saw Jack and Vince sleeping, Vince with his arm wrapped around his older brother's stomach. Lucy resisted the urge to look down and examine her clothes; she didn't want to know how dirty she was, and she knew the pale lights of the car would make it all clear. She didn't dare look out the window. The fog outside and the light in the coach would make a trembling, distorted mirror, a dark glass that might just show her what was wrong. So Lucy watched only the shadows jumping along the steel rim of the bed, and kept a peripheral vigil on the bodies beside her.

More than just her knees ached. Starting at the back of her head a thread of dull pain ran into her and surfaced like stitchery along her body. At the base of her neck the ache didn't quite rise to the surface but ran along under her skin. It seemed to be connected all the way down her back so that she could recall the feel of the boxcar's rib pressed against her. There was one sharp pain at her hip. Then the thread unraveled and ran in every direction and into both her thighs. But the distinct pain surfaced again, just where her legs joined her hip and there it seemed embroidered into her skin, and deeper. Finally, it left her body through her knees.

"Where'd you get so dirty, Mom?" Vince squinted at her and sputtered out the words. He was leaning up on an elbow, looking over his sleeping brother. At first she was angry that he didn't know. Why didn't he?

But then Lucy only raised a finger to her lips and shook her head no. She said nothing and the boy's head sank down into the pillow. He was instantly deep down in sleep again, if he had ever been awake. She wondered then if she would ever sleep again.

With a tinge of fear, she sensed that familiar glare on her. Lucy was sure the eyes of that old woman, that Corallis Bean, were examining her and trying to pry into her thoughts. She was afraid that gaze might lift her out of her seat, and set her floating again. She was afraid she might start to fly again, burst right through the roof of the car. It didn't matter if the whole rest of the coach was watching her, if only that one pair of glowing gray eyes left her alone.

She glanced over her shoulder quickly at the woman, this woman with an old Bible always clenched in her right hand, who'd been staring at her ever since they'd left Rock Island. Then Lucy looked again, more slowly this time. Corallis Bean just sat silently reading the Bible in her lap. By the position of the woman's shoulders, Lucy could imagine her iron finger guiding those powerful gray eyes across the page. But those eyes were ignoring her. And everyone else was too.

All around the coach people were sleeping, or reading, or staring out at the fog. As if nothing out of the ordinary had happened. No one was paying any attention to anything outside his own tiny world. Everyone was worrying about how he looked to someone else and no one was noticing the creaks of the floor or the thin line of dust that shaded the wall beneath each seat. It was a whole car full of little worlds, as neatly packed as if they were in separate wooden crates. Not one of them could possibly care, she thought.

That was when she noticed the trickle of blood running down her shin. She felt it inching down like an insect. She was afraid in a few minutes shed be dripping blood on the floor. She stood up then and, reaching back, she saw a tiny blood stain on her dress where she'd been sitting. Suddenly she felt dirty all over; the grime in her hair was unbearable now, and her dress was full of filth.

She walked down the aisle to the bathroom, thinking she could clean up by herself, and they'd leave her alone. Only Corallis Bean looked up at her as she walked past the old woman's seat. Lucy hurried down the aisle, afraid of those eyes that could lift her off the floor. She had nothing to hang onto, and it took all her will not to run. When the door shut behind her, the small restroom was totally dark. Lucy sat down on the stool and held her head up with both her hands, resting her elbows on her knees. Without knowing it, she began to weep. She was tired. So tired that the dirt her hands could feel in her hair didn't matter. The darkness was warm and the air was stuffy, and the room was like the old trunk. Like the cedar chest that sat at the foot of her parents' bed. It was black and quiet and empty.

So Lucy lay down on the floor of the bathroom. It was hard and comfortable, though it smelled like moldy bread. She curled her knees up against her chest and wrapped her arms around them. She laid her head down on the floor, and slowly she stopped crying; she remembered there was only one way into the trunk and with her hand on it, she could keep it shut. With her free arm she reached up and grabbed the knob, and held the lid closed. With it dark and quiet, and the lid shut tight, she could fall asleep while the train sped away into the fog.

In her dream she came out the back door of the drugstore downtown, and across the little stone bridge, and up on a hill she could see the white sandstone walls of St. Brendan's. The sky was darkening for rain, but it grew blacker and blacker, and when the wind blew up she was running toward her family's church. A thick black funnel fell gently out of the clouds and sliced through St. Brendan's from one end to the other like a butcher knife through pale yellow butter. Then she was standing on the church steps, shattered glass in a rainbow spread around her feet and a hard cold rain that smelled of urine fell from the sky. Out of the fissure in the church stepped an old, gray haired woman dressed in brown sackcloth robes like a monk. Like Saint Brendan the Navigator. The woman coughed with the same rasp as her mother did when she was dying of the consumption.

"All this way," her mother said, shaking her head. "The whole way. And we're busted. We been there. We've seen it. And we're just busted." She spit at the ground, and then she coughed. "But we seen it," she said. Her skin began turning gray as the raindrops struck it, then black, and after that, for the rest of her life, Lucy Mahon could remember nothing more of that night.

*

It was in a two-bit station in Joshua, Texas, just ten miles south of Fort Worth, that they heard the news. The fog was lifting, and Robert and Ike stood outside the freighter, stretching their legs, still talking about what the Switch Man had told them.

"I think even Lucy was encouraged," Robert said, remembering her arms around his waist.

A short, wiry man sauntered up to them. Then he stopped a safe distance away. His eyes were sunk deep into his pocked brow, and his speech was slurred with born ignorance and alcohol. "Boy," he yelled. "Say, boy. You hear the news?" He held a newspaper in his hand, but by the way he showed it proudly, gesturing at it in general, without quite knowing where to point, it was clear he couldn't read the words that were so important to him.

"You hear the news yet, boy?" he said. His eyes scanned up and down Robert Mahon, trying to perceive why he stood there beside Ike Waters.

"We got us a new champeen, boy. What you think of that?" The man's head jerked forward on his neck and then tilted to the side. His eyebrows reached for his hairline, as he asked Ike again, "You hear that, boy? Jess Willard done set that nigger down for good. Down there in Cuba. It took him twenty-six rounds, but Jack Johnson's been beat, boy. We got us a new champeen. And this one's a *real* champeen."

Robert watched him, but Ike never let on he understood. It must be a trick he'd learned long ago, and practiced hard for years. "They say he looked up at the sun, you know, the way a nigger will when he's tired and won' work no mores. That's when Willard chopped him down, boy. When he caught the nigger looking at the sun."

After the train had pulled out of Joshua and was heading south again, Ike Waters sat in silence inside the freighter and shook his head sadly in disbelief. "Well, Isaac," he muttered to himself, "welcome back to Texas."

Later on, when it was raining hard on the rail car and there was a chill in the air, Robert and Ike passed a bottle of cheap Louisiana whiskey between them. For a time, it made the night seem warmer.

Trying to kill the mood, Robert said, "Maybe it was fixed, Ike. He just got tired of it, you know?" Waters tilted the pint bottle back. "Maybe Jack Johnson took a fall," Robert said.

"No sir," Ike said, and tossed the empty bottle out the door, out into the empty night. Over the rattle of the freighter they couldn't hear the glass breaking on the rails.

"No sir," he said, "No sir." Like a chant to ward it off. Then the old man muttered something more, but Robert couldn't make it out. Hard as he tried to listen, he couldn't make it out.

The Masque Of The Intrepid

Addendum: Missing Persons Report
Case #35618-26/Hanson

This morning, with the proper court injunction and permission of Mrs. Judith Hanson of Baltimore, MD, the subject's mother, the apartment of Mr. Henry Albert Hanson was opened and an investigation of the premises was pursued by Det. Lt. Wilson and myself.   Mr. Hanson, as was explained in some detail above in the case file, was reported missing on April 29, 19--, by Ms. Candace Bowers, the subject's "friend" (as she put it).   His last known whereabouts are in Dar Es Salaam, Tanzania, aboard TWA Flight 475.   Though he had booked it in advance, Hanson missed his return flight. His trail disappears in Tanzania.   Proper authorities have been notified there, as well as in the M.P. Bureau in Nairobi, Kenya.

The Hanson premises were found in good order, with no signs of struggle or violence. All clothing and personal belongings were stored carefully in appropriate places, as though Hanson was preparing for a long vacation.   Everything was, to put it succinctly, ship-shape.   Mr. Hanson is evidently an orderly man.   Perhaps military or religious, though none of the trappings of either type of life were found. A few topographical maps of

Eastern Africa were left rolled up at the foot of his bed. The bed was carefully made, tight hospital corners and all.

As I said above, everything was in good order in the apartment. There was only one oddity. On his kitchen table we found an empty porcelain bowl, an open book, and a sheaf of loose leaf paper sealed in a manila envelope.

The book, a volume in the *Library of America* series, was left open to page 848. A ribbon marker lay across that page. This was evidently left open for us to find. It is the beginning of a story by Edgar A. Poe.

I'd suggest Detective Wilson and any other officers working on this case look over this story. It's pretty short and it may provide the key we've been hunting for on Henry Hanson's disappearance.

What follows is a typescript of the text of what Hanson, apparently, wrote on that sheaf of paper, sealed in the envelope, and left sitting next to this volume on his kitchen table. There was no address or name on the envelope.

I had the text typed up, though a photocopy of the original is in the file. It's hard to get through, because the handwriting is pretty erratic at times. Ms. Bowers and a psychiatrist friend of Hanson's, Dr. Lawrence Whidbey, helped me figure most of it out, though some of the words are our conjectures. They of course identified it as Hanson's handwriting. Ms. Bowers retains the original, though I told her it was evidence. She promised not to destroy any part of it, so I let her keep it. I know

that's not procedure, but when you read this, you'll
see why Ms. Bowers wanted the manuscript. I think
the Department can trust her on this. Besides, we've
got copies, and it's been dusted for prints already.

signed,
Inspector Gordie Pym

#

I am afraid now. After talking to Candace this morning, finally it has hit home. It seems now like this curse has struck all my friends, at least all of them that matter. All the people I'd call daring. The explorers, you know. The adventurers, the globe wanderers, the whole crew of us, now cursed. Some mad monster of fate is laughing at us, and all the while building up a brick wall around me down in the catacombs he calls a wine cellar.

And all he really offered me was a drink. A lousy taste of some fancy, old wine. The wine of daring.

It was bad enough with Diki, and then with what happened to Bobo and LaRue. But when it came to Candace, it's more than I can take. The bricks are laid up above eye level now, you know. And I'm afraid. Just call me Fortunato.

Candace was the one who named us, Diki and Bobo and LaRue, and me. She called us all the Intrepid. And she was right, too. Back then, we were fearless and bold. Nothing held us down. We picked up the name and, because of her, we began to think of ourselves as kindred souls. You could call us a school, I suppose, even though we're all so very different: Diki with her marathons, Bobo with his music, and LaRue with his schizos. We all seem so different on the surface. But Candace saw through the superficialities. At the core, our hearts were kin and she saw that. We were the Intrepid. And here's to the Intrepid Ones, Candace, all over the world. I tip to them my cup.

Because Candace is one of us too, of course. That's how she saw the truth. Candace and that wonderful body of hers.

Cheers to the Intrepid.

I pour red wine, cheap jug wine that's no Amontillado, into this coffee cup now. It's bitter and tastes terrible, but it's all I've got. The vodka gave out this morning when Candace showed up outside, her dark, pretty eyes looking blank. She was wearing running shorts, and oh what legs she has. When she walks, you can see the long muscles moving in her thighs.

When I saw her walking up the street, before she got close enough for me to see how pained those pretty eyes were, I got excited. It was always exciting to see Candace coming. And after all, we were in the season of Mardi Gras.

She is the original discoverer, the finder of new worlds. She is the conqueror of strange continents. I shudder at the thought of the places she's taken me. But for her, the whole world is held inside her body, and its especially held in all those places down between your legs.

She is the Christopher Columbus of love, my friends. Of physical love. And there are times when

Candace could make me believe the physical and the spiritual really are one thing. And that's what makes her one of the Intrepid.

So, naturally, I was excited to see her.

Every now and then, without any warning, and usually at ridiculously inconvenient times, Candace shows up ready to take you along on her voyage. If you don't drop everything and join in the journey, she's gone and there's never any returning. But if you get swept away, if you let yourself go with her, it's . . . well, let me tell you about the first time she dropped in on me.

My mother was visiting. She'd come for the weekend, to try to talk me out of my next climb: Denali. People die on Denali, you know. Dozens die, in a bad year. In a good year, the mountain barely takes a handful. Two or three. Still Mother had come running when I announced my plans: It was time for me to climb Denali.

It's a hell of a mountain, that one. Because it's so far north, so close to the pole, way up in Alaska, some say it's the most dangerous climb in the world. It makes all of the Alps and Mt. Rainier and the whole of the Andes seem easy. Even the Himalayas are safer, in some ways. Because it's up in Alaska, so close to the Arctic Circle, Denali can change on you in a moment. The weather up there can be harder than anything you'll find even on the slopes leading up to Everest, so it's a challenge that's unique. One of the few I had left, I thought.

But my mother knows about Denali. Since I started climbing in the Tetons more than two decades ago, she's learned to study the mountains I've claimed as my own. She's read more guides and perused as many topographical maps as I have, just trying to keep ahead of me. She wants to know what she should worry about, I guess. And I suppose she knew, just as I did, that sooner or later, Denali was waiting out there for me.

I tried not to tell her, but she's too sharp for that. Probably she took my silence for preparation to climb in Alaska. I couldn't fool her for a moment. So Mother flew out here, hoping to talk me out of it, knowing she couldn't, all the while. Still it was something she had to try.

I was looking out the window, and she was saying something like, "There are a lot of other mountains in the world, you know," when Candace came striding up the walk. "You haven't scaled them all, Hank. What about Mt. Hood?" Mother said. "Or Shasta?" I didn't answer her, because I was headed for the door.

Candace was smiling at me and leaning on the bedroom door. She had one knee turned out so I could admire that golden thigh of hers, and she knew I would.

"Well, it looks like I'd better be going," Mother said.

"I don't mean to chase you away, Mrs. Hanson," Candace said, though of course that's exactly what she meant. She turned a little in the doorway, and never lost that hungry grin as she gazed at me.

"No, no," Mother said, searching for her purse. "You and Hank have some things you need to talk about. He's planning on climbing that mountain in Alaska, you know, McKinley," she said.

"Denali," I said.

"Oh really," Candace stepped over and stood little closer to me than was casual.

I still couldn't believe how bold she could be. It was obvious to anyone in the room, meaning my Mother and me, that Candace didn't have talking on her mind. But she went right ahead, pressuring my mother out of the room, grinning limpidly at me the whole while.

"I've got some shopping to do," Mother said. Later, when I was clearer headed, I realized Old Mom figured she couldn't talk me out of Denali, but maybe little Candace with her golden thighs could. Candace looked a little less dangerous than Denali to Mom. A little.

Before Mother was even near the door, Candace had taken me by the wrist and led me into the bedroom. She didn't close the door behind us either. She just went for my belt. I think all my clothes were in a heap on the floor, before Mother's voice startled me. "See you," she said, and the door closed behind her.

*

Where Candace took me, that first time, was a least as high as old Mount Denali. And like the artist she is, it took her hours to lead me up to that peak. I don't even remember it all, but I know somewhere around the summit she was straddling me upside down. I had my lips and tongue tasting that golden skin around the muscles in her thigh, while her labia majora were nibbling my ear and whispering secrets I still haven't understood. I've had people blow in my ear before, but never like that.

Mother came back with sacks of wool sweaters and gloves for me, and found us sleeping naked on the still-made bed. Candace never woke, or at least she never lifted her head. Mother smiled in at me, and pointed to the shopping bag she'd hauled home. "These are for you," she said, without so much as a blush. She blew me a kiss but didn't step through the doorway.

Then she left. She flew back East that very afternoon, comforted to know I was safely in the sack with a sweet, if a bit wild, young woman. If anything could keep me off the alpine turf of highest Alaska, it was Candace. That's what my mother reasoned.

But she didn't know Candace.

Wrapped up in the sheets, we ate a dinner of warmed over Chinese, and then Candace was gone. With just a little kiss on my forehead, she smiled and left. I don't think I saw her again for six months.

*

Despite Mother's wool gloves, I lost one of my little fingers on Denali. The cold of the glaciers on its north slopes took a couple of my toes as well. But I stood on the peak, where I could see all the world below my feet, and I grinned at the little touch of death we call frostbite. I'd made it again. Fear was still the greatest enemy, I told myself, and I'd beat him again. Beat him in his own country, where he held the high ground.

But these days I just look out and try to see the dark sky above all the bricks that the madman heaps up about me. Now I'm afraid. Montresor is his name, he tells me.

It came to Diki first. Bobo and Candace brought me the newspaper with the story in it, and sat with me while I read about her.

She was great in her stride, you know. She was the best. And what a will she had, Diki. It was hard not to love her when she ran. She was taller than me by almost a foot, and made of long lines filled with the tension of wound spring. She could run all day, I thought sometimes, and still at nightfall have the strength to sprint that last hundred meters. It was a beautiful thing to watch, the way she ran. And she always ran best when she was challenged.

And I don't mean by another runner necessarily. I remember watching her once in Arizona, in a grueling desert race, twenty six miles at the foot of Oak Creek Canyon. The last mile climbed up onto the walls of the Canyon. It was a course designed by a sadist, I think, and more than a few runners failed to finish that marathon. Most who did came across the line at the pace of a slow walk. It wasn't only the course, either. The weather was cruel too. Though it was scheduled in the winter, the sun broke out hard that day. It reached the nineties on the thermometer, but on that black asphalt it must have been over a hundred. Runner after runner doused themselves with water, and it just seemed to dry off of them in moments.

But there never was anyone like Diki, in her prime. Candace and I saw her at the midpoint of the race, striding along with a pair of other runners. They were in the lead by a few hundred yards. But she was the one who was beautiful: The grace of those long, fleet steps, holding back their real speed, and that sharp tilt of her chin high in the hot, still air, her brown eyes had that fire of challenge in them. It took my breath away to see her easy stride when she ran along the road. The two women beside her were fighting against themselves. Already a fierce grimace of struggle on their faces, and an uncertain stagger to their step told you they would end up at the back of the pack far behind, if they finished at all. But not Diki, she was in her stride, just beginning to see her limit, miles and miles out in front of her.

Candace and I rode ahead then, on a rented dirt bike across back roads up the canyon, and we waited for her at the finish line.   This is what I remember most.

She came to that last, cruel rise in the course, after 25 miles in desert heat, and she was alone. Everyone had fallen far behind.   The crowds along the course were waving and cheering and chanting out her name, because they knew and loved her the way we all did.   She could have walked it in and won, maybe with a record.   Certainly with a record for this course.   But that fierce grimace, the one we'd seen ten miles before on her long lost competitors, it was there on her face now.   Her step was staggered and a little less sure.   The run had been harsh, even on Diki.

But her eyes rose to see that last 400 or so, switchbacking up the canyon walls, and I swear a grin floated to her lips.   I think it was the last challenge she was grinning at, the one that weariness and pain and death were throwing at her, the one all the other, mortal runners could never face, and she enjoyed it.   She grinned right in the mad mason's face, I think, and then she kicked it out.   Diki fairly sprinted up the canyon road.   It must have made the sadist who designed the course scratch his head.   It made the rest of us cheer.

She raced across the line and then stood, black arms akimbo, her chest heaving the desert air, glowing in dark sweat, and she laughed.   Not at winning.   That was old news for her.   She was used to it.   No, she was laughing at the threat in those last hundred meters, and the way she'd conquered them. She was one of the Intrepid, after all. And Candace and I were at her side, laughing too.

She was kicking the mason's wall down and scattering the bricks around us all. So she laughed, and I laughed too.

But I never saw her last race. Even if I could have known it was her last, I suppose, I wouldn't have gone to see it. I want to remember her as she was that day in Arizona, on her way to medals and honors and championships galore, laughing triumphantly.

I read the article in the paper as Bobo and Candace waited silently. It was as a race in Colorado, a high mountain marathon near Aspen that ended in Glenwood Springs. As she came to that last fifty meters, downhill toward the Hot Springs pool, Diki fell. She had to crawl across the line to finish the race, still in first place.

"That's right when she usually kicks it," I said. The others nodded.

"No one seems to know why she tripped," Bobo said. "She says she wasn't tired; she still had lots of kick. But suddenly, she couldn't feel her feet anymore."

"That happens," I set the paper down. "Diki told me sometimes, when she holds her head high at the end of a race, she feels like she's looking down at herself. Out of body, you know?" I was thinking of what it's like to stand on a mountain peak and look down. I shook my head at the thought, but didn't say anything. "Then she couldn't get back on her feet?" I said.

"She crawled the last fifty feet. After she tried to stand up, that is," Bobo said.

"And she's still not walking, Hank," Candace seemed more upset than the rest of us. She may have been the first of us to see the brick wall going up. I don't know.

"Well, what is it?" I said.

Candace could only shake her head no.

Bobo was the one to explain. "There's no broken bones or torn ligaments or anything else they can see easily. Everything seems to be in good shape. She just can't walk."

I took a deep breath and felt the anger rising in me, anger at the crazy injustice of it. "How is she holding up?" I said.

Bobo shrugged. This time it was Candace, the one who'd called us all Intrepid, who put the words to it.

"She's afraid, Hank."

Over the next several months Diki saw every kind of doctor there is, I think. Including the shrinks. They tested her blood and her heart, her spinal fluids and her nervous system, her bones and even her head, her poor head. Inside and out they pried at her and poked at her, and came up with nothing. They called it MS and MD and CF. They ruled out Lou Gehrig's and Dr. Graves' diseases. They even tried psychotherapy, and later on hypnosis. In the end, they could tell her only two things:

They didn't know what it was.

It seemed to be spreading.

We went to see her everyday that we could, when she was well enough to be seen. I held her hand and felt how cold it was. We talked about how it would be when she got better and she'd resume training, when she'd be running long distances again. We watched the Olympic trials on the TV in her room. Eventually, we began to talk about coaching, about how much she could offer to young runners from her wheel chair. And she seemed strengthened by that, and by the daily therapy that taught her how to manage in a walking world from a chair. That sprinting to the finish spirit was still there. Diki wasn't giving up. But I noticed what wasn't there: the laugh.

Oh, Diki laughed and joked around. But the real laugh, the one we'd shared at the finish line in Arizona, that laugh in the mad mason's face, it was gone. Gone like the legs she'd once used to kick down his walls. Gone with her long, sweet stride. Gone like the heart that used to beat in her chest with the rhythm of a great river. Just gone.

"I can't take this anymore today," Candace whispered in my ear. Her face was whitewashed of all emotions. But with a toss of her head, she led me out of the room and we left Diki with LaRue. It was evening at the hospital, the hallways were dark and empty of everyone but muttering nurses who glanced up at us and smiled vaguely as we left, or ignored us altogether.

She led me down a hall to the elevator, and then got us off on some basement floor. She seemed to know where she was going. She must have been scouting around the hospital, or maybe she was just lucky. Maybe she was just lucky. Maybe she as just looking for anywhere, and found it. Through a busy lobby she lead me to a door and, without glancing around, disappeared inside. I did the glancing and it looked like no one saw us go in.

It was some sort of examination room, I thought, and Candace was already rooting around in the cabinets and drawers when I quietly latched the door behind us. "Get on the table, Hank," she said without turning around.

"I just don't know what to say to Diki anymore," I mumbled, as I hopped up on the padded bench. It was black but covered with a strip of white paper pulled from a roll at the end of the table. "It all makes me so sad, Candace."

"Lie down," she said.

I was starting to get excited because I realized Candace was about to take me on one of her voyages of exploration. I hadn't seen it coming, I was so wound up over Diki's demise. The last thing on my mind was sex.

"Are we going to play doctor?" I chuckled, as I stretched out on the examination table.

Candace didn't answer, she just closed one cabinet and opened another below it. "Ah ha," she said.

"Shouldn't I get undressed, Doc?" I said, with a laugh of anticipation. But then I realized this was Candace's response to the crazy fate that had felled Diki. The only way to confront the fear in Diki's world, for Candace, was to turn around, pick up a compass and head off in a new direction. I was the new direction tonight. At least for now. It made me feel sad, but unaccountably so. Not for myself, or for Diki. Somehow for Candace.

She turned around then, hiding behind her back something she'd found in those cabinets.
In moments she had my legs up in the stirrups above the table. It happened almost before I knew it. I guess women, with all those years of visits since puberty, they know how to latch up those high straddling braces.

"Now, Mr. Hanson, let's have a look, eh?" She removed my pants and underclothes, easily, one leg at a time.

Then she brought out what she'd been hiding from the start. The restraints. They were made of foam and Velcro, with cloth ties. While I laughed at her, she bound my wrist to the table, and then my feet she bound to the stirrups up in the air. "Now what?" I said, as I tugged gently at the soft restraints on my arms.

Candace just laughed and stepped away across the room. I looked at her from between my two bound feet. I saw my missing toes, the ones I'd lost when I stared down the mad mason on Mount Denali. I was wearing nothing now but these foam restraints and a cotton shirt. "I want to study your attention span, Mr. Hanson," Candace said with a laugh.

"Whatever you say, Doc."

But I didn't realize what she meant. You see, she moved up then and stood there just between my legs, though not touching any part of me. She didn't even touch the examination table. Slowly, as she watched me for any reaction, she began to disrobe. Her sweater and a scarf around her neck came first. She was, oddly, sort of business-like about it. Even when she kicked away her shoes and dropped her skirt, there was nothing of the striptease about it. She was a scientist, watching me spread eagle before her. Any response I might have had was stifled by the cold room and the brittle paper under me that rattled every time I twitched. Not to mention the way I was still chuckling and tugging at the restraints with good humor.

Then she looked up at me. She was standing there in just a lacey pair of bikini shorts and a slight bra, but her eyes were what started it. She looked up at me with a hungry gaze, and even if it was contrived by her "science," I felt the fire kick in, all down my spine.

"Oh, I see, Hank," she smiled. "Lace and anatomy isn't enough for you. You need attitude as well." One of the straps on the bra dropped down carelessly, and she shrugged her shoulders so it fell lower yet.

"Candace," I said, "I don't know if I like this." But I was nice and erect now.

She kept those eyes on mine, and unhooked the bra, let it drop to the floor. Her breasts were soft and low slung, and I was not.

Watching me carefully the whole time, Candace began to work me over without touching anything but herself. First the bikinis were gone. Then she touched her own nipples so they blossomed hard. Taking her time, she played with herself until she was hot. Or at least she acted that way. I'll never know for sure.

It was all slow and sweet in the craving. The frustration drove me harder and harder, but I was bound hand and foot. She was careful never to touch me with anything but breath and body heat. Before long I'd sweated through the paper underneath me and was begging her to finish me off.

She kept me there, aching like that, for what seemed like hours though it was probably countable in ticks of the clock. Then finally, I guess she gave up, because she leaned over me and wrapped my erection between her breasts. That was as much as I could stand. "Sorry, Candace," I said, assuming we were still just started. I spurted all over her chest and my stomach, and I think I let out a groan.

But that's when the applause broke out.

I looked up and saw a row of windows across one wall, and they were filled with what must have been med students, male and female both. This gallery was cheering and applauding our little show, and roaring with laughter now too.

I suppose I turned deep red. But Candace, she just stepped back, took a deep bow like the acrobat she was, scooped up her clothes and gracefully slipped the skirt and sweater back on as she headed for the door.

"Candace," I said. "Wait. Don't leave me here, like this."

She stopped, smiled at me, untied just one of the restraints, the one that held my right wrist down. Then without a word, she tossed her blonde hair back, blew a kiss to the gallery, and was gone.

One of the residents, who came down to help me get loose, said, "Ballsy lady, huh?"

I laughed and toweled my embarrassed stomach off. "Fearless," I said to him. "Totally fearless, Doc."

The curse of Fortunato fell on poor LaRue next. He was probably the last one of us I ever thought would fall. But he was the next.

LaRue was a therapist, and something of a renegade at that. Now maybe you don't think it takes courage to do therapy, and maybe it doesn't when you're dealing with pimple problems in the suburbs or with academics who've read too much Nietzsche and lost their will. But that wasn't where LaRue worked. Anorexia and divorce counseling weren't his game.

LaRue was a believer in the old idea, crazy though it maybe, that you can't cure madness. You just learn to manage it with a dose of acceptance.

To put his ideas to the test, Larue had taken on the toughest cases he could find. He wound up in the state's penal system, counseling lifers. Now some of these guys have hard breaks and bad luck along with their character flaws to blame for their prison terms. But there are others. LaRue deals with them too, the guys who talk regularly with flying saucers and dead pharaohs, or even worse, with God and the saints.

These are the folks LaRue hungered for, the real challenges. It takes some guts, you know. Especially when you believe, like LaRue does, that you've got to talk to them straight. Take those murderers and rapists with no hope of ever seeing the outside again, with nothing left to lose because they've already lost it all, take them off the sedatives and give those wild heads free rein. LaRue says, "My only goal is to help them accept their delusions for what they are: madness. Instead of chemically numbing them until they're tomatoes, let 'em run with it. Then maybe they can learn a delusion is a delusion, not a calling or a commandment."

So, on a daily basis, LaRue goes in and sits in a locked room and talks to the craziest of the crazies. And they love him for it.

But it takes some guts, I'd say.

I admire him for it. I always say to him, " What you do, LaRue, it makes Mt. Everest look like a footstool, my man."

He doesn't buy it, but it's true.

Or all of this was true until the day of the Frisco quake. LaRue was out at the San Lucia

Center, locked in a room with some serial murderer. He told me he was sitting in a chair and the patient—he always called them "the patient"—was walking nervously around the room. The patient was describing the way he knew the time had come to kill the latest child he'd been stalking.

"You see, Doctor, I'd stalk one or another of the kids, a little boy or girl, and all the time I was asking 'Is this the one?'" The patient put his hands flat on the plastered walls. "Sometimes I'd go for a long while before the earth told me. Sometimes I'd have good chances, just a little kid in a park alone, just waiting to be snatched. But the ground didn't speak. So I had to wait."

"Were they always children?" LaRue asked.

"One time, just once, there was this young woman in a wheel chair, and I stalked her for a while to see, but the ground never spoke. So it wasn't her. Other than that, Doctor, it was just kids."

Fourteen of them, in fact. That's what LaRue told me, sitting in my living room staring down at the floor, his hands trembling as he spoke. "This guy grew up in the suburbs of Chicago, Hank. He started stalking little kids in high school, in Oak Park, but it never came to anything, so nobody noticed. Somewhere, the chemistry in his brain led him to believe that he shouldn't kill, even if he wanted to, not until the ground told him to kill. So years went by and he never told anybody that he was waiting for the earth to speak. He went to college, got a degree in engineering and computer science at Northwestern. Got married. Got divorced. No real problems, you know? Nothing out of the ordinary. And then," LaRue stopped to laugh at the irony of it. "Then his company transferred him to Northern California."

Right near a fault line, as a matter of fact. Over the following five years, he stalked children as he always had, but now the earth began to speak. And so "the patient" began to kill. Every time there was a tremor, he knew this kid was one of the "lucky ones." Fourteen times in five years, before he was finally caught.

"It was a perfect case for me, Hank." The trembling spread up into LaRue's shoulders, as he spoke to me. "Instead of sedating him, instead of drugging the crazy chemicals out of his mind, I just had to teach him what a damn earthquake was. He was always going to hear voices in an earthquake. I think he was always going to believe they were talking to him too. But I thought I could teach him to talk back to them. He could learn to tell them he wouldn't do what they said."

"This guy would never get out again," I said.

"Of course not, not after what he's done," Larue said. "But if this theory of mine worked with him, then maybe he could live in that prison without being drugged into a stupor. Maybe he could do something fruitful with his time in there. And more importantly, if it worked with him, it could work with some others. Maybe we could help some people, less violent cases, we could help them live fruitfully, if not sanely. We might even catch someone early, before they heard those voices say 'kill.'

"It was the perfect case, Hank," LaRue said, still not able to look up at me. He shook as if he'd been overtaken with Parkinson's Disease. "Just like I'd been searching for. That 's why I'd spent so much time with him. Until . . . "

Until the big quake hit that October. LaRue was in the room with "the patient" when the whole prison complex began to shake. The patient stood there, his palms still on the wall, but now his head was cocked as if he were listening closely to someone. His eyes stared ahead of him blankly, concentrating. "What do you hear?" LaRue asked him. He claims he was excited by this chance, at first. "What is it saying?" But the patient just stood there, mouth gaping, and then he nodded his head.

Outside the cell, LaRue could hear people yelling and footsteps pounding the halls. The patient's eyes focused on him then. LaRue put the notepad in his coat pocket and closed the fountain pen. "Guard?" he said to the door without looking back at it. There was no answer, only more yells and running footsteps in the distance. The patient took his palms off the concrete, windowless walls.

"Did you hear something?" LaRue said to him. Then he said the man's name. The prisoner walked toward him, wiping his sweaty hands on the prison jumpsuit. "Remember what we talked about now?" LaRue said. He shoved that fountain pen down in his pants pocket, looking around on the table top to see if here was anything else he needed to hide.

"What was that, Doctor?" the patient said.

"You know, about the voices you hear."

"What about 'em, Doc?" he said.

"Guard?" said LaRue, in a yell now.

The patient lunged at him then, and they struggled for a long five minutes or so. He tore into LaRue's pocket and grabbed that pen. They wrestled on the floor as he tried to push the pen point into LaRue's eyes. Eventually the guard rushed in, pulled the patient off of him and helped LaRue outside. He was all right, except for the torn trousers and the indigo ink all over his face, but he was trembling. While the guard hurriedly sat him down outside on the floor, they heard a scream from inside the cell.

"It was a scream I'll never forget, Hank," LaRue said. "The guard rushed back in there, and I got up and looked inside, through the narrow slot in the door. It was too late. Just that moment of checking me in the hallway. It was too much. The patient, he was sitting inside that room, on the floor against the opposite wall, and there was blood all down the side of his head and his shoulder. He had my pen, Hank, shoved into his own ear. He had it shoved down three inches at least, and he was working it around, while he screamed at the pain.

"He wanted to kill the voices, Hank."

LaRue sat up straight on my couch, and he clasped his hands together in his lap, trying to stop the trembling. That tremble had been there, without a rest, ever since the day of the quake. LaRue never went back inside those prison walls. He gave up on his research entirely. He'd been doing three months of therapy himself, but he still couldn't sleep through the night. And the trembling was constant.

"I can't face it anymore," he said to me, and I wasn't sure he meant the prison, or the trembling.

"It'll get better," I said to him. "With time, you'll get your confidence back." I remembered talking to Diki this way.

"I'm never going back," he said, and there were tears in his eyes now.

I went over and hugged him, telling myself the whole while, 'We are the Intrepid.' I thought of Candace proudly naming us all. We are the Intrepid. "You don't have to, LaRue. You can leave it alone. There's plenty of other people who need help. The suburbs are full of people in pain."

"I've got nothing to say to those people," he said, and seemed to get some control of his hands again. "What can I say to them, to any of them. 'Hey, I'm afraid too. Run, baby, run. While you got the chance.'" Then he laughed bitterly at himself.

This was the man not even madness could scare. Another one of us. And now he was bricked in completely, suffocating in his grave. The mason had won again.

Bobo was the last of the Intrepid. He is a composer and he works with small groups and with chance to make great vocal structures I don't always understand. He's taught here and there, everything from piano lessons to counterpoint to music history, and he's played his clarinet all over the world, but mostly he's written music.   When the teaching begins to interfere with his composition, he's quit. And he's refused to play nightclub music or advertising jingles.   I've seen him working nights as a janitor, to keep his mornings free for him to write.

Not all his music has been played yet. Some has been done in galleries and lofts around here, or in New York and Montreal.   He's had one piece that was a minor hit in Boston, at Berklee, and some Italian record company recorded it.

Because Bobo is black, everyone calls his music jazz. But it doesn't sound like Count Basie or John Coltrane to me. Sure, it has a strong sense of rhythm, and it uses mostly horns in small ensembles, and it's always vocal even when there is no singer. He lets chance hold much of it together, so the individual musicians are part of the process of composition.   But I don't know if that makes it jazz.

For the last two years, Bobo had been working on an opera.   He's given up a couple chances to play with Richard Abrams in Chicago and turned down two opportunities to record in New York, one of them with Miles Davis. We all told him he as committing career suicide. But he doesn't care. For two years, all his life has gone into this opera, based on *The Sound and The Fury*.

Candace says it's that crazy abandon, his stubborn born will to write, that makes him one of us.   Though I don't always understand the music, I agree with her. He's fearless when it comes to his music. Right or wrong, smart career move or blind ambition, *The Sound and The Fury* will be done.

Or at least that's what he said before his time came to meet the masked bricklayer down in the catacombs. Before his time came to taste the Amontillado. Until I saw what happened to Bobo, I thought LaRue had it hard.

It was around this time I began to plan my ascent. I know now it was because of what had happened to Diki and LaRue. I didn't know yet what was coming for Bobo. I'd watched what had befallen them. It was time for me to climb up and above, to look down on the planet and to stare all its many evil fates straight in the eyes, and laugh at them all, the mad mason included. It was time for Africa. Time for Kilimanjaro.

I went to REI and bought the maps first, then I made a few calls and began to put together the team of guides and climbers I would need in Tanzania. Kilimanjaro is not the toughest mountain in the world. It's ten thousand feet lower than Everest. But it has its own, storied challenges. Especially the way it stands alone, rising thousands of feet above the plains of East Africa. Sometimes it's not how high you are at the end, but how far you've climbed to get there. Kilimanjaro rises alone over twelve thousand feet from its base. And then there is the weather.

Like Denali, Kilimanjaro is a special challenge because of its weather. Because it lies so close to the tropics, only three degrees south of the equator, the mountain is almost as changeable as the Brooks Range far north of Denali. But instead of the dangers of frostbite and blizzard, Kilimanjaro is 19,000 feet of avalanche and flash flood just waiting to haul you away and turn your body into a twisted, broken heap of brush at the base of some rocky gorge.

But it was what I needed just then. Maybe when she saw Diki crying in a wheelchair, Candace wanted to teach a bunch of residents how the Kama Sutra works. But for me, when I saw LaRue trembling in fear, I wanted Kilimanjaro. And I wanted it in the height of spring, deep in the rainy season when the waterfalls are blasting on the rocks and the mounting spring snows are heavy with melt, leaning off every cliff, piling up with the eternal rains, waiting for that unnecessary yell or that meaningless slip to set them roaring down. Waiting like an evil man in a black silk mask, down in the catacombs, during the madness of carnival.

I was at the track in the gym, running wind sprints, getting physically ready for Kilimanjaro when Candace showed up. "Hank," she said. Usually it would be a thrill to see her, you know, but lately I'd been seeing her mostly in hospital lobbies or at LaRue's apartment. So I didn't know whether I should expect a voyage with her, or just more bad news.

I leaned back against the wall of the gym and caught my breath. "I'm going to Africa," I said to her. She handed me a towel, and I wiped my eyes and forehead, draped it around my neck. In a moment more, I breathed out, "In April."

"Africa?" she said.

"Kilimanjaro."

She took hold of the ends of the towel around my neck, so she had me. "Is that a dangerous one, Hank?" she said, smiling at me.

"No," I said. But I told her about the rainy season weather and the danger of early spring slides. She was quiet then.

"Is everything all right, Candace?" I touched her finger on my towel. "You got any news for me?"

"Everything is fine," she said, sounding not so sure of herself. Then she said, "Lets go, Hank."

"To Africa?"

She laughed. "No, silly," she pulled on the towel and drew me toward her. Then she kissed my sweaty brow.

"Let me get showered up, and then . . . " I said.

"Hank," she looked at me with those dark eyes that meant business. "Lets go," she said.

She picked up the shoulder bag she'd been carrying and led me outside in my gym clothes. There was a cab waiting, and when we got inside, she was still holding that towel around my neck. The taxi took us to the Olympic Hotel downtown.

Candace led me straight through the lobby and upstairs to a suite. It already had the Do Not Disturb tag hanging on the door.

"You had all this planned," I said.

"No, Hank," she laughed at me. "I keep this suite rented all the time, my dear. You just haven't been her before."

I almost believed her.

There was a king size bed, already turned down. But first she led me into a shower. I undressed her as she undressed me. Since I was only in gym shorts and a T, I thought she'd have me naked before I figured out how to unhook her bra. But I pulled off her knee length raincoat, and I could see immediately that she wasn't wearing a bra. In fact, as I loosened the strings of her harem pants, I found out she wasn't wearing any underwear at all. We laughed at one another as we kissed and soaped each other up in the shower. Before long, I had a mouthful of soap from licking at her wet breasts, but I didn't care.

Inside the king size bed, I was licking the remains of red lipstick off her upper lip—it was the last thing she had on—when it occurred to me this was all too traditional for Candace. We were headed for the missionary position in a hotel afternoon, and that was just too old fashioned for Candace. At the same time I wondered where she was taking me on this voyage, and I wondered what was wrong.

But I didn't wonder for long.

She stopped kissing me and leaned down to retrieve her bag. Then she scooped out a whole handful of condoms, followed by another handful. There were some with ribs and spines, and some with little nipples on the end. There were all kinds of colors, some that glowed in the dark, and some that needed a black light to really show their stuff. And then we had different oils and scents to choose from. She may have had two dozen of them there. I was afraid to count.

"What do you want to start with, Hank?" she smiled at me. "Lemon yellow or orange orange?"

I picked out one wrapped in foil with the word "Tickler" glittering in two colors, and said, "Let's try this one for a laugh."

"Funny," she said. Then she bit the foil open with her teeth. The way she slowly unrolled it and put it one me, while I played with her, almost finished me for the day. But she seemed to know right when to stop. "Candace," I groaned, but she was already back in her grab bag of tricks.

The next one was fluorescent green with a lime scented oil. She called room service for whip cream and a fruit basket. While we waited for the food, we made love with the "Tickler." Then, after answering the knock at our door wrapped in our king size sheet, and leaving me naked on the bed, she made desert on my stomach and ate her way toward that lime glowing in the dark.

Afterwards, while we rested in the bed, she wanted to know how it was for me. Did I like the Tickler or the flavors? Which was better?

I thought we were done then, and I couldn't help it: holding Candace in my arms, I began to think about all the work I needed to do before I was ready for Africa in the spring. But Candace wasn't finished with me yet. She rummaged around in her collection of socks and came up with a model she called her pina collada. It was a ribbed deal with coconut oil. I didn't think I had it in me, but as the sun set outside over the Sound, and she began to kiss my stomach, I began to taste the sweet coconut in the back of my throat.

We spent three days like that, calling room service for food and accessories, making love in all positions, and always with a different flavor of protection. Candace worked us slowly, delightfully through her whole collection. When I thought I would be sore and incapable, she was always gentle and ever resourceful. I lost track of time, and completely forgot the Mountain, and all I can say is when we finished the whole collection, and finally slept for long, indiscriminate hours, I woke ahead of her. She was exhausted, I think. Her mouth hung open, and she breathed deeply and silently. I woke her gently by making love to her, simply, without any props or shields. Her eyes glowed with love that last time. I suppose mine did too.

When we finally put on our clothes, they seemed like a lie or a betrayal. They seemed soiled and ancient, and they didn't fit.

Not long after that lost weekend, Bobo was flying back from New Mexico. He'd had a gig in

Santa Fe, at some new music festival in the mountains. He'd played instrumental highlights from the opera with a sextet of other musicians at the festival. Someone there, one of those wealthy industrial heirs hoping to get her name emblazoned on the dedication page of the manuscript or on the wall above the museum entrance, had liked his work. There was talk of mounting a full production, in year, at Musique Actuale in Victoriaville. Bobo was up all night for a couple days running then, he was so excited: he called Candace from the airport to tell her the wonderful news. He had a patron.

And then Montresor bought him his ticket, and began to lay the bricks around him on the plane. Bobo never saw them building up around him jealously, until it was too late. Jealous fate.

Probably it was the lack of sleep for starters. He let himself get run down. And there was the change in climate too. Those high, dry mountains above the desert air. At any rate, Bobo caught a cold.

But he had to get back. The manuscript of the score was waiting, now with the funds to finish it Bobo popped an overdose of antihistamines into his system, hopped on board the plane, and fell asleep in his seat. Somewhere over Utah the piercing pain in his ears woke him. They were plugged and full, and with a crackle that could be heard in the seat next to him, they popped. Then he stumbled down the aisle and threw up in the little washroom at the back.

Must be all the cold dope I took, he thought. He had trouble getting back to his seat, because his head was throbbing and he felt like he was at sea, like the plane was tossing in the waves. A flight attendant helped him back, and buckled him in. He was dizzy and nauseous the rest of the flight.

Candace and Diki picked him up at the airport, in a mood to celebrate his good fortune. Diki was in her wheelchair, and it turned out to be handy, because Bobo was so unsure of his step, he wound up sitting in Diki's lap all the way out to the parking lot. They laughed all the way, balancing Bobo's clarinet in his lap while Candace tried to push the wheelchair straight on through the crowds. Then Diki sat in the car and massaged Bobo's temples, while Candace went back for his bags.

"I'll be all right," he said when the two women wanted to take him straight to see a doctor. "It's just this stupid cold. It's giving me a headache you can't believe." He laid down weakly on his couch. "I just need some rest, you know. Then I'll be able to get to the score. Tomorrow, I hope."

But tomorrow didn't dawn that way. Nor the day after. Diki wound up staying over the first night, he was so weak and helpless. The headache wouldn't retreat, not even under a barrage of painkillers. But even worse, his sense of balance kept rocking him all night. Every time he tried to close his eyes, the bouncing of the room around him made him toss up the painkillers, along with the orange juice and chicken soup Diki kept feeding him. The only way he could rest was by staring out the window at the smooth horizon of the Sound, steadying his gaze there while the room rolled around him as if it was a ship on the high seas. They were up all night.

I brought him some Dramamine the next day, when Diki called. It was left over from a deep sea salmon fishing trip LaRue and I had taken, once long before, in better days. When Diki described his symptoms, I thought maybe the stuff would help. It knocked him right out.

We sat with him in shifts, Candace and Diki and I, for the next two days. "It's just this stupid cold," he'd say from the couch when he was awake. The Dramamine and some Motrin kept him out for most of the time. Diki stuck with the soup and the juice, right after the Dramamine worked. By Wednesday his cold was almost gone, but we barely noticed, because the room still moved around him and he said his head ached like a bowling alley on a Saturday night.

The doctors, once again, were mystified. Diki laughed ironically at that, and then later she wept about it. Bobo had done something to his inner ear, they said. Then they started on the round of tests that seemed so familiar to me now. They did everything but stand him on his head and twirl him around. And I think that was only because no one suggested it. After two weeks in the hospital, they sent him home. This was their only advice: "Learn to cope with it."

Once Bobo was home, in his own place, the final bricks in his wall were set in place. He thought maybe he could get back to work, a little at a time. His world still rolled like the high seas, and while that made driving impossible he decided he could live with it. But then he discovered the real curse, the little twist of the trowel that the mad mason had waiting for him. It waited until he was home, and until he grew used to the prescription and the patience it took to live without a sense of balance. Then the real pain began, slowly, to rear its ugly head.

At the slightest sound above the volume of a whispering human voice, Bobo went spinning in agony to the floor. Any loud noise, and his head seemed to split wide open. He learned quickly that he needed to live in near silence.

We moved him out to the foothills, Candace and I, to a little solitary cabin. It was quiet out there. We tiptoed around and spoke in whispers. And once we made his world quiet, he heard Montresor seal the last brick into place. There was a ringing in his ears. A constant, variably pitched whine that covered up our whispers, and all the soft sounds. He could function with us, speaking quickly, but he was always in one of two situations: piercing pain and nausea at some loud sound, or listening carefully and quietly through a constant whistle in his ears.

"It sounds like someone with a piccolo is always practicing the high register on my shoulder," he told us.

But here was the last brick. He could hear no music. If we put a symphony or an opera on, he had to constantly adjust the volume to only one dynamic, turned low enough so he had no pain, but not high enough he could truly hear it over the piccolo concert in his ear.

"I think I remember this happened to Smetana," I whispered, trying to sound encouraging. "Didn't it?"

"Hank." Candace shook her head at me.

I shrugged back at her, and then Bobo laughed bitterly and explained her frown. "You forgot what it did to him, didn't you, Hank?" His laugh grew a bit louder, and then he winced at the pain. "It drove Smetana mad, Hank," he whispered after a moment. "He even tried to use it, you know, he put his ringing in his last quartet."

"I always hated that piece of music," Candace said later, after we'd all sat in silence for a time. "With that hum in it, at the end, in the last movement, that string quartet always seemed so . . . " She searched awkwardly for the right word, the safe word, and couldn't find it.

"Pitiful," Bobo said finally. Through the sealed bricks around him.

Over the next month or so, he began to see an acupuncturist, and a dentist began to replace all the fillings in his teeth. The doctors thought maybe his bite was wrong, and when the new fillings didn't fix his ears they started to talk about breaking his jaw and setting it differently. Bobo persevered through it all, but I'm afraid the music in him disappeared.

"You can still write the score," I said to him once. "After all, look at Beethoven, he . . . "

Bobo held up his hand to stop me. "I can't compose without my ears," he whispered. Then he lay on the couch and wept soundlessly for a while.

He didn't have it in him, at least not then, to scream back at the mason. Maybe he couldn't bear the noise and the clanking of chains inside the little cell Montresor built around him. About a week after that, he wrote to his patron and told her of his plight. "Give the grant money to someone who can use it," he wrote. "Let's not spend it on useless doctor bills." And so his *Sound and Fury* fell silent; it came to nothing. He began to spend his time reading comic books and sleeping too much. He put on thirty-five pounds. He whispered a lot abut physical therapy, and didn't laugh much anymore.

But I couldn't stand it. I'd had enough. It was time that someone, some one of us, the damned Intrepid climbers, it was time one of us yelled back at the mason and his evil bricks. It was time for one of us to protest, not to just fall down in the chains and give up. Candace and I were the only ones left, but I couldn't wait for her. It was time for me to yell back.

I called Tanzania, and I moved the date up for the climb. And then, while I was on the phone, it occurred to me. I would do it by myself. I would climb Mt. Kilimanjaro alone. So I cancelled out of the team, and chose only a pair of bearers.

On the mountain this time of year, about the last four to five thousand feet of the ascent will be ice and snow. Soft and loose from the African summer. Deep and heavy from the monsoon rains. That is the stretch I will climb alone. The bearers can wait for me while I do that last, treacherous ascent up to Kibo all alone. Then I will stand on the summit, looking down into the crater of that young volcano, and yell out all the curses I know at the brick walls mounted around my dear friends. I will laugh in Montresor's face, and kick down the foundations he was trying to lay around me, and around Candace too. And maybe when Diki and Bobo and LaRue hear my rebellious yells, when my victorious laughter rings in their ears, maybe they'll rise up out of their ignominious chairs of defeat, and find the strength to poke a hole in the walls of their tombs. Maybe all that crazy bricklayer needs is a good yell and a shove, and he'll leave us alone.

"But isn't that dangerous, Hank?" my mother said. I didn't laugh at her on the phone. I would save my laughter for Kibo, the peak of Kilimanjaro, when I flipped my finger at old Montresor and his trowel.

No, I just told my mother a lot of comforting half-truths. "It's not as bad as it seems," I told her. "The guides will be waiting just a few thousand feet below the summit where our base camp will be. They'll know how long it should take me to make the top. And they'll know my route exactly. Both up and down, Mother. If anything goes wrong—and it won't—they'll be right there behind me in just a few hours."

All of that was true. But I carefully didn't tell her that what I intended to do was to take the southwestern route to the summit. The guides would think I was going up on the safer, north face, the traditional route to the top, but I was going to slip around to do the rock face, under Malewesi, to the southwest, so I will have to climb almost a thousand feet up out of the crater. A thousand feet of snow and rock loosened by the African sun and primed by the African rains to slide. I would cross that secretly alone. Truly alone, without the help or knowledge of the bearers. This one was all mine. And only mine.

"Hank?" my mother said. "I don't know if I believe you." She could always read me.

"Mother, don't worry," I lied. "After Denali, this will be a cinch. A cakewalk, Mom. I could do it blind."

It was Diki who seemed to respond the quickest when I told her. "That sounds very dangerous, Hank," she said. Then she grinned, pounded her fist on the arm of the wheel chair, and flipped me a thumbs up. LaRue, I think, was too confused within his trembling to really understand what this ascent of Kilimanjaro meant for us. "It's for all of us," I said to him, and he nodded at the floor, his hands clasped like he was praying for the shaking to stop. Bobo was so lost in his pain and the loneliness it left him in, I didn't think he heard me when I whispered my plans to him. I told him everything softly, even the things I neglected to tell the others: from the dangers of flash flood and avalanche, right down to this lone, secret ascent up the southwest face, and into the deep crater. I have to admit, I think I told him so much because I thought I was talking to myself the whole while. He seemed not to hear a word. But as I spoke, I felt the fire of defiance flaring up on the fuel of my blood. Bobo's unshaved face was blank, and I was sure he'd been hearing only the whistle in his ears as he fought to hold the nausea quiet and calm in his guts. But when I stood up to leave, and nodded my thanks to the home health nurse, Bobo grinned at me. "The Intrepid," he whispered, through clenched teeth.

Candace I couldn't find. I called around and stopped by her apartment, and I even went to her suite at the Olympic and disturbed some steel haired gay couple in the middle of the night. Candace was nowhere to be found.

I spotted her out my window on the morning of Mardi Gras, walking up the street toward my place. The sidewalks were still littered with the confetti of the night's celebrations. It is the season of abandon, I reminded myself.

She was wearing running shorts and a sweatshirt in the brisk, late winter rains. Her blonde hair was wet and her bare thighs were covered with goose bumps when I greeted her at the door. "Aren't you cold?" I said.

"I was running," she answered, but she seemed distracted.

"Let me get you something to warm up with," and I went into the bedroom and brought out a heavy terry cloth robe. She was still standing in the doorway when I came back, and I put the robe around her wet shoulders and said, with a lusty chuckle, "I'll warm you up, Candace." Then I hugged her body to mine and began, again, to wonder what she had in store for us today.

"I think you should get out of those wet clothes," I suggested. I could feel her hard nipples through her sweatshirt against my chest.

But she just wriggled out of my hug and strolled over to the sofa. "Do you have anything to drink or smoke?" she said, flatly.

She knew I stayed away from pot. It was too hard on the lungs, at least after all these years, when I was above twenty thousand feet and hanging off a rock face. The cost of smoke was too much then. So I gave it up. But she was distracted, and must have forgotten. "Some vodka," I said, "I think."

I got the bottle of Stolichnaya down with a couple of tumblers and a shaker of paprika. I brought them out to the sofa. "You want juice or water or anything?" I said as I watched her pour herself half a tumbler and then down it in a couple of kid gulps.   She sat looking at the empty glass, and shivered a little as the alcohol settled in her.

I poured myself a finger or so, then with a dash of paprika I made a Bloody Natasha, and tossed it down.   With the taste of the paprika lingering on my tongue, I sat next to her and touched her wet hair.   Someone told me once, it may have been Candace, that paprika in a good vodka was an aphrodisiac.   I could see the brown back of her neck, with the strands of her shining gold hair sticking to it.   She smelled of rain and sweat when I leaned over and kissed that bare spot, above the collar of the robe.   Then, as I rubbed her back, feeling every vertebra and then the softness of her waist, I told her about Kilimanjaro.   Though for some reason, I didn't tell her I was going to scale it alone.

She didn't say a word, just poured herself another hefty dose of vodka.   Then she sighed deeply, and with my hands I felt the breath flow in and out of her.   It made me hot in anticipation.

I saw her, in my mind's eye, the way we would be in a moment or two.   My eyes took away the old robe, and the running clothes beneath it.   I saw her breasts from the side, touching the little folds in her stomach.   The nipples were pointed, and around them a rosy pink halo the color of paprika was waiting for my lips.   I thought maybe this time it would be my experiment.   Could I bring her to the peak of ecstasy just by kissing and tasting those sweet breasts?   This would be my gift to Candace, my farewell challenge before I climbed back to the summit for all of us.   For the Intrepid.

I let my hand slip down along her side until I could cup the roundness of her breast beneath all the terrycloth and cotton. I was talking all the while about the peaks of Kilimanjaro, and how I was going to conqueror them all, stand on the summit of Kibo, for us. For Diki and Bobo and LaRue. And for her. Then I moved even closer and held her, and I slid my other hand up under the robe and her sweatshirt and with a grace that rarely comes to me in such moments, I undid her bra. As I kissed her cheek, my fingers grazed along the sweat and rain in the wrinkles of her stomach, and then I held that full breast. "I'm going to laugh in his face," I whispered. "Laugh in the face of Fate."

But Candace was unresponsive. She sat still as if she was curious about how she might react to my overtures. Then, after it was clear that there was no response in her, she just wriggled away from me. She pulled the old, baggy robe around her, like some hag in the street outside a mission. Then she stood up, taking the bottle and tumbler with her. She left the paprika alone on the table.

"Well, while you're up there," she slowly sank into a chair across the room from me, "laugh at this, will you." Then, without going on, she poured herself another tumbler of vodka. I saw pieces of motley colored streamers and confetti stuck to her shoes from the rainy carnival streets.

"What's up, Candace?" I said. All my desire for her was suddenly swept away by the first, small wave of fear. The first of many more to come, I'm afraid. I didn't want to hear what she said next. Not from Candace. Not from the woman who'd given us our name.

She took a deep swallow from her tumbler and then said, "Its over, Hank." That blank look came across her dark eyes again. "It's over." For a moment I thought she meant us, but then we had never really been an "us."

"You don't have . . . " I couldn't bring myself to say it. "You're not . . . ?"

She laughed and looked over at me. "No," she stood up and came to me.

"No, I'm negative, Hank, but . . . " She set her glass down on the coffee table and laid her hand on my cheek. It was hot and moist. " . . . that's just it, isn't it?" She poured me a good double shot, and then shook her head and sat down beside me again. But now I was not imagining her bare breasts kissed by my lips.

"It's just not the same anymore," she said, and began to sip on the vodka as she spoke. "No matter what I do now, it's all ruined. Everyone's afraid, Hank. There's no spontaneity anymore; everyone is thinking of protection and my whole life feels like its covered with latex.

"The adventure's over, Hank. We're all worried, we're all thinking, all the time. 'What will this mean?' we say to ourselves. I can hear it out loud in everybody's thoughts. The way we act, it screams at me."

She sighed a deep sigh I'd never heard from her before. "There are whole worlds left to explore, Hank. But everyone's afraid to go. I'm perfectly healthy. Every part of me is fine tuned, and eager to run. But my life is over, Hank. It's over and done with."

"But there are ways to . . . " I said.

"I tried, Hank. Believe me, I tried." Candace sank back into the sofa, clutching the Stolchinaya to her chest. "I tried them all. You, of all people, know."

I remembered our lost weekend then, when every color and flavor she could find she'd wrapped around me every way we could imagine. Suddenly, that lost weekend didn't seem so lost. It was a last desperate search for a way. The bricks were building up around her too. That lost weekend was carefully, desperately planned. Little, if anything, was spontaneous up there in that hotel suite.

"It just doesn't work anymore, Hank." She looked up at me like we were talking about a lost marriage, "It's over."

I didn't know what to say to her. I was trying to understand it myself.

"It's like every mountain in the world," she said to me, "has got a set of escalator stairs. And if you want to get to the top, and not take the stairs, you can't find anyone who'll dare."

"I will," I said to her.

"But that's not the problem, Hank. The problem is," she took a deep breath, "I won't."

*

So we drank until the vodka was gone, and then she left me the robe and the paprika, and walked away in the rain, with the confetti and bits of streamers still stuck to her feet.

But for us the carnival was over. It had happened to Candace too. She had let herself be chained up in the catacombs, and she watched in her motley garb of bells and patches as he slowly built up the bricks around her. She knew, just like Diki and Bobo and LaRue, that Mardi Gras was roaring on, in the streets above where he had buried her, but there was nothing she could do. A madman, with just a smile and a story, had chained her to the wall.

And so, I am alone. There is only me and Montresor left. All the rest of us, the Intrepid ones, are buried beneath his heavy, black bricks. There is only one Fortunato left. And the hole that remains before him in the mason's brick wall has a name. It is called Kilimanjaro.

So I sit here tonight drinking this red wine out of a coffee cup, alone, listening to the sounds of Carnival in the streets outside. And I wonder what to do. What if I try the mountain, alone, and fail? What if I don't come back? What if I disappear into the wastes of Africa like some latter day Rimbaud, and find only the death and disease of my end? There is a good chance of it, after all. I'm not young anymore. I don't have the strength I had once, on Denali and in Nepal. And even there, I needed help. Now I'm soft in the middle, now matter how many miles I sprint, no matter how many weights I rack up on the machine. The strength I've clung to, I suppose. But my endurance is gone, it won't last in the extreme. The expanse of my chest only hides the weakness inside me. My endurance is gone.

The more I ponder it, and stare at the maps of this rock face laid out at the foot of my bed, I know I won't come back. Maybe it is just the wine and the vodka I started with this morning, maybe they are doing the talking now. But I know I won't come back. Because I'm afraid, you see. And sure as the hell in Montresor's eyes, that fear will kill me. At just that moment when I need to hang tough on the rock, when the pylon slips in the granite, or when the rope begins to fray at the rock's edge, that moment when I need to be cool and calm as steel, the fear will kill me. It will flay me like a lost desert flower against the rocks. Because I'm afraid.

That's why I sat down here, poured more wine in the cup, and began to write this chronicle. Because if I don't come back. No, when I don't come back, I want to leave this for Candace and the others. They should know, even if no one else does, why I scaled to my death in the heights of Africa. Why I took it on alone. They should know about Montresor. But if I don't come back, if I plunge in some hole on the side of Kilimanjaro or if some slide buries me under an ocean of snow, hasn't Montresor won? Isn't that, after all, what the Mason in his madness wants? He wants us to fail, in our fear. Or does he want us only to give up in advance, to fail for not trying? In our fear.

For a long time tonight I've tried to tell myself that. The way to win is to be careful, to play the cautious card and not lose the whole deck. And it wasn't hard to see how it could all work out, because it made sense that way. It was just common sense, that's all. I'd been talking it all along, see. It's what I've been telling the others for months. It was time to take my own advice.

Diki would press on with physical therapy and the tests, and there were schools and even the Olympic team where she could coach. Maybe she'd even run again, someday, since I know, she has the heart.

For LaRue, it was time to put it all down on paper. Maybe he'd lost the will, but he had the information. And the patient with that pen in his ear had learned at least to distrust the voice in the earth. He was trying to kill it, after all. So it was time for LaRue to write those theories down, with all that he's learned and experienced. And maybe, when he'd been through it all in his mind and ordered it down into print, maybe then the trembling would stop and he'd walk back in there, walk into those cells again, but wiser now. Ready for the earthquakes to come.

And for Bobo. Yes, it breaks your heart to lose something you've developed to such a perfect pitch. But that was, after all, what had come to Diki and LaRue, and now to Candace too. Bobo could learn to read the scores, he could lean to write music with the inner ear that was even deeper than the ears trying to destroy him now. He might never hear the music he wrote, but his heart didn't have to be silent. Not for one of us.

And most of all, I suppose, I saw the answer for Candace. Just like it was for Diki and Bobo and the rest, old Montresor had tossed her the ultimate challenge in the form of a curse. It was time now to choose one partner. It was time to make the new worlds of her senses hot for a lifetime exploring one small place, to fall in love with that one place, and let it become the doorway to worlds within. The adventure of loving forever, not for everywhere. The real challenge was to love deeply enough that, yes, finally the physical and spiritual did meet, they were one, in us.

I saw that for Candace, and I hoped I could join her there. I was ready to go with her again, but this time to the most dangerous journey of all. The journey that takes a whole life, because it swallows all the time you have. And maybe it goes beyond that, too.

And I was ready, I told myself. We were the Intrepid, after all. We didn't need me to die on Kilimanjaro. The way to defeat that crazed man in the catacombs was for all of us to take the challenge at hand, to accept the curse of Fortunato.

And so, for me, there was the climbing school at Paradise. It was time for me to accept the weaknesses beneath my tough, trained shoulders, and to give the gift of the mountain tops to others. I didn't need to climb alone. I could stay home, with Candace, and learn to care for my friends. That would be the great act of courage. To learn how to bolster them, so we could be the Intrepid again. In a new way. Battered with our fears, beaten by the fates, but intrepid again. The Intrepid still. Once and for always. The Intrepid.

That sounds like wisdom, doesn't it? Writing it down makes it all sound like truth, especially when it follows on that bottle of Stolchinaya we drank this morning.

But it's dark out now; the streetlights are on, and I'm loaded with cheap red wine. I can hear the sound of the Carnival in the distance, the street bands and the dancing children. I know they're wearing masks and that soon the morning light will come. And then the streets will just be littered, and the jobs will be waiting. Yet in the dark, tonight, the garbage and the day's work are not in sight, so all the children dance as if there was no morning. Still they're wearing masks. And I know why.

Because they know that Montresor is waiting for them, dressed in black and wearing a mask too. But he' not a reveler, he's a mason. He has a job to do. He wants to lure them down into the place of the dead, that lies beneath the very streets they're dancing on.   And there, in the dark, with the promise of a taste of the sublime and the secret, he'll trick them into his chains and then, while they watch, he'll brick them in.   The wall will close around them.   It doesn't matter what bells and funny hats they wear, what motley colors decorate their souls, or how they've taught their deepest songs to dance in the darkest light, he will bury them alive.   And then, like he always does, he'll place the bones of the dead—they were revelers once, too—around his bricks to hide the wall he's built.   And you know, and I know, whose bones they are.   Those are the skulls and the empty rib cages of all the dancers who came before, all the dancers and singers and magicians the mad mason has tricked before.   The catacombs are filled with their gypsy remains.   They are the somber, dark parade of Carnivals past.

     And Montresor?   Who is he?   Where does he lie?   He's the mason of the morning, the architect of rush hour and deadline, of paycheck and mortgage, grand marshal of all the holiday parades, lurking down in the catacombs beneath our dancing feet, so the streets aren't safe at night.   You must not go down into the dark with him.   You must wear the Mask of the Intrepid, and dance for all you are worth.   Don't listen to the promise of Amontillado. Don't trust the safety of what lies beneath your feet. Dance upon it.   Dance through all the daylight. And into the ever Dark.   You must.

He has taken Diki and Bobo. LaRue is in his grasp. And now even Candace has lost her soul to the catacombs. She's set down her mask and held out her hands for his chains. And of the Intrepid, there is only one left to keep up the dance.

That's why I leave this now, beside the text of Poe. I seal it and set it here, to be found when I don't come back. I am afraid now. But because of it, I put the bottle of wine away on the shelf. For the training is done. All the preparations are complete. It is earlier than I'd planned. But that is of no matter, because there is only me. The last Fortunato.

Tomorrow I go to Africa.

#

Addendum: Case #35618-43, M. P. Report/H
Hanson

May 17, 19--.   Though Henry Albert Hanson
remains missing, the cables from Dar Es Salaam,
Tanzania, indicate the M. P. Department there finds
no sign or trace of the subject.   His trail, effectively,
ends at the airport.   It is not known whether the
subject continued on to the Mt. Kilimanjaro region.
If he did, he evidently traveled under an assumed
name.   I think it likely Mr. Hanson disappeared in
the mountains on the Kenyan border.   If he in fact
survived his trek, he has chosen to remain missing,
in effect to disappear.   Therefore, it is the judgment
of this inspector that the status of this case be left
open but no longer pursued, and that Mrs. Judith
Hanson and Ms. Candace Bowers be so informed.
                    Signed,
                         Det. Lt. William Wilson

A Note about the Author

Sandro Dariosto now lives part of the year in Emilia near Ferrara, Italy. He is author of THE LAST GOOD RUN, BURTON THE RED and THE WISDOM RUN, as well as Jazz journalism for sundry magazines.

A Note on the Type

This book was set in Iowan Old Style, a typeface designed in 1990 by John Downer, who was inspired by serif typesetting originally created in Italy in the 1490s.

This book is a publication of

p.s. *A* Edizione

per sempre Anita edizione
Via delle Scienze, 17 Ferrara 44100

www.ingramcontent.com/pod-product-compliance
Lightning Source LLC
Chambersburg PA
CBHW051413170626
46809CB00006B/2139